GALÁPAGOS BELOW

A QUINTERO AND HOYT ADVENTURE

D. J. GOODMAN

SEVERED PRESS
HOBART TASMANIA

GALÁPAGOS BELOW

ISBN: 978-1-925493-64-1

1

Out of the six passengers in Ernesto Padilla's panga, five of them fell into a reverent hush as they approached Isla Niña. The sixth, Debbie Schmidt, didn't speak either, but the look on her face made it clear to Ernesto that this wasn't because of any sense of awe on her part. She'd probably just tired herself out with all the complaining on the ride here. Everyone else in the boat, her husband included, seemed grateful for her silence. It meant they could enjoy this moment in peace.

So, of course, she had to wreck it. "I still don't see what the big deal is. It just looks like someone took a giant shit in the ocean."

I will not throw my paying customers overboard, Ernesto thought. *That would be unprofessional.* Although he wouldn't be surprised if any of the other tourists cheered as he did it. Even Bernie, her husband, had begun to look like he'd had enough of his wife's whining by the third day of their week-long trip. Ernesto wasn't even entirely sure why the two of them were here. The other four people in the panga were biology students, here because, for them, these islands were their closest thing to Mecca or Jerusalem. Bernie Schmidt seemed to share some of their enthusiasm for the Galápagos Islands, but his wife had refused to participate in most of the activities. Instead, she usually preferred to stay back on the main yacht and turn her skin from pasty white to tomato red. Bernie had convinced her to come with them for Isla Niña, even though Ernesto had subtly tried to tell him that maybe, out the five islands on their itinerary, this one was hardly the best for her.

In a way, Debbie Schmidt was right about Isla Niña. From a distance, it looked like nothing more than a mound of brown and black, completely uninviting and not appearing to host any life. That was the amazing thing about the Galápagos Archipelago. To humans, they were hostile, barren, many of them devoid even of fresh water. That was part of why they had been left alone for so long. That was part of why they had been able to thrive in their own unique and beautiful way.

Debbie groaned as they got closer to the island. "Where's the dock?"

"There is no dock," Ernesto said in his heavily accented English. "I said before, this is going to be a wet landing."

She stared disbelievingly at the black volcanic rock that circled the island. There was no flat beach on Isla Niña, just the jagged rocks hanging between three and ten feet over the surf. "Where's the stairs then?"

"No stairs," Ernesto said. "We will tie off the panga at a low point on the cliff and climb up."

"Climb?" Her voice rose to a hoarse shout. "You can't be serious."

"That's the only way to get up onto the island."

"You can't expect me to climb anything. This is my vacation."

"You could stay in the panga, if you want."

"No, I insist you take me back to the yacht."

There was a collective groan from everyone else in the inflatable raft. Mrs. Schmidt seemed thoroughly surprised that she was the only person who thought this was unfair.

"Why aren't there stairs?" Mrs. Schmidt asked. "Or a ladder?"

Ernesto thought he had done well so far in maintaining his cool. He was responsible for these people, after all, and silly little blow-ups could put them at risk when they were floating out upon the ocean. He had to admit, though, that even his well-known calm started to slip.

"There has been much effort to keep the islands as natural as possible. Any sort of permanent structure on the island could affect the wildlife."

Mrs. Schmidt mumbled to herself, something about wildlife knowing its place or something like that, but she didn't say anything more, nor did she try to get him to turn the panga back around. Maybe, just maybe, she would behave herself long enough to learn a little appreciation for the island.

They had needed to arrive in the morning to take full advantage of the day and the light, but that had the unfortunate added effect of making them approach Isla Niña when it was coming up on low tide. At high tide, any climb would be easier, since their handholds would not be as slick from the retreating waters and the water would be higher up the steep rock face. He'd come to Isla Niña enough times now, though, that he was aware of the best landing spot even at low tide to provide his passengers with an easier way up. He maneuvered the panga into a shallow alcove of rock where the cliff hung closer to the water. This was where the sea lions were most likely to congregate, although for some reason he didn't fathom, there didn't seem to be any basking in the sun here today. There were, however, a number of marine iguanas feasting on the algae-covered rocks, and he stopped the panga long enough for a couple of the biology students to take their cameras from their wet-dry bags and snap a few photos. One young woman cooed over a larger specimen, noting the way it bobbed its head, and correctly identified that as a sign that it wanted to mate.

Mrs. Schmidt ignored it all, instead staring back in the direction of their yacht some distance away.

After the students had taken their fill of pictures for the moment, Ernesto instructed them on scrubbing their shoes with brushes before going onto the island. Isla Niña had been completely off limits to anyone other than scientists up until recently, meaning that out of all the islands the Galápagos Park allowed people on, Isla Niña was one of the most unsullied when it came to invasive species. Most of the tourists already knew the drill, although of course Mrs. Schmidt scoffed at the idea that her expensive hiking boots could somehow cause any damage to the tiny island's ecosystem. Ernesto, still not showing his growing impatience, gave her the talk he'd given everyone else when they'd gone to previous islands—that anything, even a tiny seed from one of the other islands, could cause a radical change in Isla Niña's unique pool of flora and fauna. She didn't seem to understand or care, but eventually she scrubbed the bottom of her shoes with a stiff brush just like everyone else.

"When I get home, I'm going to need a vacation from my vacation," she said.

"And I'm going to need a divorce," Bernie whispered, not to anyone particular, although he was close enough that Ernesto could hear.

"What was that?" Debbie asked.

"Huh? I didn't say anything," Bernie said.

Once the panga was tied off, Ernesto helped the others up onto the least steep part of the rocks. The marine iguanas, displaying their famous lack of care for all things human, made no effort to get out of the tourists' way, forcing them to use some fancy footwork to get around the creatures. For a moment, as Bernie was helping her up the rock, Debbie looked like she was about to purposefully kick one of the iguanas. If that happened, Ernesto would have no choice but to take them all back to Isla Santa Cruz immediately and end the tour. Any attempt to intentionally harm the animals was illegal, and he could be held accountable if he didn't enforce those rules. Her foot slipped before she could do anything, though, and she scraped up her hands and arms as she scrambled for purchase. The rough black rock could be almost glass-like in the right circumstances. Even though he hated himself for it, Ernesto felt a small amount of joy at the idea of this woman bleeding. Any blood that fell would need to be cleaned up, of course, but Ernesto was willing to do it if it finally meant she was going to stop making things so difficult.

Once everyone else was up the slope, Ernesto followed, spider-climbing up with the ease of much practice. Finally, they were on Isla Niña, and Ernesto couldn't help but smile as all his tourists (short of Mrs. Schmidt, of course) stared around themselves in wonder.

Again, to anyone who didn't know better, Isla Niña wouldn't have seemed like anything worthy of a second look. The ground, rocky in most places and reddish in the few places that could actually be considered soil, was home to only the scrubbiest-looking plants and grasses. Further in on the island's three-mile radius, they could see a few cacti, but the average person still wouldn't recognize any of this as special. Only when they paid closer attention would someone notice the scrawny variety of scalesia, an alien-like flower distantly related to the sunflower, growing in a few clumps. On one island, the scalesia had evolved into something the size of trees, but Isla Niña's breed stayed small.

"This is seriously what we've come all this way for?" Mrs. Schmidt asked. Her husband ignored her, instead caught rapt by the sight overhead. The biology students, too, stopped everything to stare. Overhead hundreds of blue-footed boobies circled, and nearby a number of great frigatebirds joined them. Ernesto recognized most of the frigatebirds as female by the white coloring of their necks, but those weren't the ones that got everyone's attention. Instead, it was the male frigatebirds, their red throats swollen up with air like bizarre, fleshy and feathered balloons. Ernesto smiled. It must be mating season for them.

Bernie's gaze move downward to where something else flittered and caught his eye. "Wait, is that...?" He pointed at something about the size of his palm, a small dark shape that zipped through the air and landed on a cactus.

"Yes, it is," Ernesto said.

The biology students oohed and ahhed. Mrs. Schmidt raised an eyebrow. "Just looks like a bird to me."

Ernesto would have corrected her, explained why this one little finch meant so unbelievably much to the Galápagos Islands, not to mention the entire history of biological study itself, but she wandered away before he could say anything. Her path was technically forbidden, as tourists weren't allowed to go anywhere other than on designated paths, but Ernesto let his duty as a guide slip for the moment. Let her be miserable elsewhere. These other people had paid him to take them to, what was to their mind, an ancient lost paradise, and he wasn't going to let one person ruin it for them. And so he ignored her, instead choosing to carefully creep up to the cactus and explain the specifics of the tiny finch they were seeing.

"So, that's one of the famous Darwin's finches, right?" Bernie asked.

"Yes. Specifically, this is a small cactus finch. Each of the finches are endemic to specific islands. While some types can be found on multiple islands, this one only exists here, on Isla Niña. An entire species of bird that only exists within a three-mile radius, and that's it."

Ernesto went into his typical spiel about what made the Darwin's finches unique, specifically their beaks. The biology students nodded sagely, most of them apparently already knowing most of this, but Bernie Schmidt ate it up the most. Ernesto had to wonder how someone like him had ended up with someone like Debbie Schmidt, but he supposed that wasn't any of his business.

"Amazing, isn't it?" Ernesto said. No matter how many times he went over this with tourists, he still felt some awe even in himself. "Such a small creature. And yet when Charles Darwin found them, it changed everything we knew about nature and the world."

The cactus finch tweeted at them, more annoyed at their presence than afraid, and flew away. The tourist group, apparently satisfied for the moment, broke up and milled around as Ernesto checked all their supplies. They would be here for a couple of hours before heading back, and while that might not seem like a lot of time, the amount of supplies he had ready for it was great. He had food and blankets and first-aid supplies, enough that they could stay the night if something went wrong. He'd never had that happen, though. He'd been a licensed guide in the Galápagos long enough that he could head off most emergencies long before they happened.

Which reminded him of Debbie Schmidt. Her hands had been scraped on the climb up the slope. While he was more concerned about what her left-behind blood might do to the ecosystem than he was about what she might get infected with, he still needed to disinfect any small wounds she might have.

When he looked for her, however, she was gone.

Ernesto had a brief moment of panic before he brought himself under control. This was no worry. He'd had tourists wander off before. On some of the larger islands, that might be a problem, but Isla Niña was so small that he should be able to see her no matter where she was if he found a high point. He was more concerned that she could have wandered too close to the edge, slipping on the algae and loose rocks to plunge into the ocean.

He told the biology students to stay put and get ready for lunch, then pulled Bernie Schmidt aside. "Did you see which way your wife went?"

"Um, that way, I think," he said, pointing a slight distance away.

"Let's go get her," Ernesto said. "She will probably listen to you more that she would to me."

Bernie made a mirthless chuckle. "Debbie listens to herself and her mother. Sometimes, I think I actually catch her arguing with herself if she doesn't have anyone else."

"Still, come. She cannot be wandering around the island by herself."

The two of them went off in the direction Bernie had indicated, both of them silent at first. Once they were a distance away from the others, though, it was like the tourist sprung a leak in whatever held his quiet in.

"I know what you've been thinking this whole time. You've been wondering how I put up with her."

Ernesto certainly had been thinking that earlier. For now, he was more concerned with getting the group all back together. They were well off the trail now, and if certain authorities knew he was leading tourists off the approved paths, he could get in trouble. The animal life on the islands had a tendency of getting underfoot, to the point where boobies would build nests right in the paths, unaware that such a move might put them in danger of being squashed. If Mrs. Schmidt accidentally stepped on and destroyed something important, not only would Ernesto likely lose his permits, but Isla Niña would once more get closed to the public. Considering the uproar some environmentalists had unleashed over opening a new island to the public, Ernesto suspected any such accident would turn him into a non-person in Puerto Ayora.

While Ernesto had been thinking on this, Bernie had still been talking. "...it was either that or her sister. And I couldn't do that, you know?"

"Um, right," Ernesto said. Then he pointed, glad for the distraction. He hadn't actually been paying attention to the tourist's words, but he suspected they contained more personal information than he wanted to bother with. "There. She is over there."

Wonder of wonders, it looked like Debbie Schmidt had actually seen something that didn't cause her to go into complaining fits. She was stooped down on the rocks, dangerously close to the edge, so close that the spray of the ocean waves misted her face. She didn't appear to notice or care, though. In fact, she actually looked like she was smiling.

"Debbie?" Bernie asked as they got closer.

"Shh," she said. "You'll scare it away."

Whatever it was, Ernesto doubted that. The Galápagos animals indifference to humans was legendary, going all the way back to the tales Darwin had told of having to push iguanas out of his way in *The Voyage of the Beagle*. Still, happy that the woman had found something on this trip to enjoy, he slowed his walk so that whatever she had found wouldn't feel threatened.

"What is it?" she asked Ernesto, her voice almost reverent.

"Uh, looks like a crab to me," Bernie said. Unlike with the finch, he didn't look terribly impressed. Funny, how he and his wife had suddenly switched places.

Ernesto inched closer to see the thing crawling around on the edge of the rock face, prompting Debbie to hold tight to the black rock if she wanted to continue watching it as it made its way back down to the edge of the water.

"A Sally Lightfoot crab," Ernesto said. The crab, only about ten centimeters long, was nonetheless a sight to see given it spectacularly bright coloring. Its pincers were small, almost stunted compared to other crabs, giving it a feeling that couldn't really be said of any other crustacean: it was almost cute.

"Who's Sally Lightfoot?" Bernie asked.

"Jesus, Bernie, who cares?" Debbie said. Her voice lacked much of the venom it had earlier. She leaned further over the edge, trying to watch the crab as it joined twenty or thirty others just below the high-tide line.

As much as Ernesto wanted to let her continue having her moment of awe, her proximity to the edge unnerved him. "Mrs. Schmidt, please come back this way. We shouldn't be this far off the path."

For a second, the glare she gave him made Ernesto think that she was going to throw another fit, but it went away quickly to be replaced with a gentle, contented smile.

Ah, Ernesto saw. That was why Bernie had married her. The islands did, after all, have a way of bringing out the best in some people.

"Okay," she said. Ernesto backed away so she would have room to scuttle away from the cliff edge. "Are there more like that on the island?"

"Oh yes." Confident that she had inched far enough away from the edge that he wouldn't need to grab her, he turned around and waved for the two of them to follow.

He took several steps before he realized that neither of the Schmidts had moved. When he looked back, he saw them both in quiet conversation. In that moment, they almost looked tender and loving toward each other.

I can give them a minute yet, Ernesto thought. He started walking toward the trail again.

Something erupted behind him. A massive spray of water hit him in the back with enough force that he fell on his face, his cheeks immediately feeling the sting of sharp black rock. The water continued to fall on him for a second, a very localized rain storm.

He sputtered seawater from his mouth, dazed from the fall. It took him several seconds before he heard Bernie Schmidt screaming.

Ernesto got to his knees and turned to face the Schmidts. Except there was only one Schmidt, now. Bernie stood about a meter from the edge, staring down at the water below. He was drenched, although it took Ernesto a few seconds to realize it wasn't just water darkening the man's clothes. There were spatters of blood as well.

"Mr. Schmidt?" Ernesto asked, then realized maybe that wasn't the name he should be calling. "Mrs. Schmidt? Debbie?"

She'd fallen in. That had to be what had happened. Except was had caused the plume of water? Where did the blood come from?

Ernesto scrambled to the edge, barely noticing as he stuck his hand in some warm liquid that was definitely not water. Bernie stayed where he was, not moving, completely frozen in place. Ernesto wasn't even sure he was breathing.

"Debbie?" he called out over the side. The water below churned for several seconds as something dark and large moved somewhere deep in the blue waters. Then the water became still.

"What happened?" Ernesto asked, standing up and grabbing Bernie by the shoulders. "Where did she go?"

Bernie's eyes remained unfocused, his face a perfect sculpture of shock. His mouth moved silently a couple times before any sound came out. "I... I... it moved so quickly."

"What? What was it?"

"It was too fast. Too much water. I didn't see. It... It..."

Bernie looked down at something on the ground. "It took her."

Ernesto followed his gaze. There, near the edge of the cliff, was a severed human left arm. Blood still dribbled from the open wound. If there was any doubt about who it had belonged to, the doubt vanished when Ernesto noticed the recognizable sun-burnt skin, and the wedding ring on its finger that was an exact match for Bernie's.

2

Maria Quintero stared at her fingers sitting in the water, slowly pruning among the greasy dishes from dinner. After a few seconds, she realized she had been looking blankly into space and tried to force herself back into the moment. The night was almost over. All that remained was dessert, and she and Kevin would finally be able to leave. She would have said that they would leave to be alone, but there was no longer any such thing for them. A small crew of camera people, sound engineers, and various other television types now followed them everywhere. The price of modern insta-fame.

Even at this very moment, catching her period of spacing out for everyone to see, there was a woman with a camera standing a discreet distance away. Charlene, her name was, and as much as Maria wanted to not like any of them, Charlene and most of the other crew of *Sea Avenger* were good, polite people, many of whom had the decency of being embarrassed at how in-her-face the producer forced them to be.

Sea Avenger. Ugh. Just the name of the show made her twist in embarrassment. Both she and Kevin had had a lot of input on the show and its content, but the title, unfortunately, had been set in stone at The Education Channel, or TEC as it was better known, when they had approached her in the hospital with the contract. With her face all over the news, ensuring she had already lost most of her privacy, along with mounting medical bills, she and Kevin had agreed.

So here they were, creating riveting television of her washing dishes. Yeah, there was a reason the suits at TEC were starting to get antsy.

I suppose I better give them something a little better to watch, she thought, suppressing a noticeable sigh. She finished up the dishes as quick as she could, then grabbed Mama's pies from where they had cooled on the counter and brought them into the dining room.

So many people in such a relatively small room. Mama, Papa, her two brothers, and Kevin were all crowded around the table. Other than Charlene following her, there was one other cameraman, Gary, the young man who had been fortunate enough to catch the footage that had propelled Maria to fame. There was also the sound engineer and boom mike operator. Susanne Merchant, the producer whom the network had tapped after the inexplicable disappearance of previous producer Doug Vandergraf, was probably in the living room right now, undoubtedly on another call with the network arguing about the footage they'd gathered so far. It was an argument that was happening more and more frequently, and one that was becoming harder for her and Kevin to ignore.

Tonight should probably make them at least a little happy, Maria thought. It wasn't the exciting, tense footage the network had thought they would be getting, but she supposed someone out there would probably think the extreme awkwardness could make for good television.

Kevin, for his part, had done his best to ignore the disapproving looks of Maria's parents for all of the dinner. He was used to people giving him weird stares when they found out he was transgender, and knew how to make it look like he was blowing it off in public. In private, of course, Maria knew just how much it bothered him, but that ability to act was what made him so photogenic, right along with why he had originally been considered as the star of *Sea Avenger*.

Then the events in the Sea of Cortez had changed everything. As much as Maria wanted to forget about it all, she couldn't. Especially at night, when she took off all her clothes, followed by her prosthetic leg, then stared forlornly at her stump before going into a restless sleep.

She hobbled to the table and put the pies in front of everyone, hoping this would trigger some semi-civil conversation. Her brother Ramon made the obligatory noises about how good they smelled, although the older brother, Felix, continued his intense brooding silence. Papa quietly said thank you, while Mama was her typical self and chided Maria for forgetting to bring a knife and serving plates. While she bustled off to get them, Maria sat down next to Kevin and held his hand under the table, a show of solidarity and a sign that this damn night was almost over.

The whole night had been Merchant's idea. Maria had known it would need to happen eventually, although she'd never expected it would happen on camera and then get edited in the most dramatic way to increase ratings. Because at the moment, there didn't look like there would even be ratings. *Sea Avenger* had been shooting for nearly a month, and there was one very important element missing. Maria was here, the titular Avenger, and there was plenty of footage of her in physical therapy, learning to walk with her new prosthetics, lots of tender moments between Maria and Kevin.

No, *Sea Avenger* had no lack of Avenger. What it was missing so far was the sea. The first episode was supposed to air in less than a month, and until they got back to the water, the network was getting antsy and doing everything they could to create drama. Hence tonight. Hence the first time her family had ever met the famous marine biologist Kevin Hoyt.

So far, by both Maria's and the network's ideas of success, it looked like tonight was a disaster.

"So, uh, this looks like a new recipe," Maria said, indicating one of the pies.

"Mama bought it at the store this time," Felix said. "This all happened with too little time for her to make it from scratch."

"Oh," Maria said. Under normal circumstances, she would have been able to say something jokey with her brother, but he hadn't said anything more than he had to since they'd arrived earlier today, well before dinner to ensure the crew had time to set up. Mama came back from the kitchen and set a plate in front of each one of them. Maria couldn't help but notice the way her mother put Kevin's plate farther away from him than everybody else, a passive-aggressive show of disapproval.

"Okay, look, can we just finally talk about this?" Maria asked. Ramon stopped jabbering to anyone who would listen. Papa sat up straighter in his chair. Charlene and Gary tensed, each of them focused on getting the best possible shot of whatever happened next.

"Whatever are you talking about, Maria?" Mama asked. Her tone made it obvious that she knew exactly what Maria was talking about.

"No, I think you're right," Papa said. "It's time we got some things off our chests."

"Okay, you know what? I have nothing to do with this," Ramon said. He stood from his seat and left the room, all excitement for pie completely forgotten. No one tried to stop him, and all conversation ceased until he was gone.

"Look, I know you both disapprove…" Maria said.

"We never said that," Mama said.

"You're damn right we do," Papa said at the same time.

"But I'm surprised at both of you," Maria continued. "I never thought you would be this narrow-minded."

"We're not narrow-minded. We have legitimate concerns, Maria," Papa said.

"No, the fact that I'm seeing a transgender man is not a legitimate concern. It's my own damned business."

Mama and Papa went silent, both of them turning to give each other confused looks. After several seconds, Mama responded. "Maria, honey, is that really what you think this is about?"

Now it was Maria's turn to be confused. "Well, yeah. You've both been so terse when you talk with me whenever I bring up Kevin, so I just thought…"

"Maria, don't you remember where we live?" Papa said, gesturing at the house around them. "This is San Francisco. Why the hell would we think it weird for you to date someone who's transgender?"

"Oh," Maria said. "Then I guess I don't understand. What is the problem? And don't tell me there isn't one, because I can tell the way you sound angry every time I talk about Kevin on the phone."

"Well, for starters, how about your education?" Papa said. "You put it on hold to do some hands-on work down in Mexico, and you haven't been back to complete it. We spent a lot of money to make sure you had this, and it's like you're flushing it down the toilet."

Kevin looked like he was about to say something, but Maria squeezed his hand and he got the hint. This was her battle to fight. He was the one that always said he didn't need her fighting his battles for him, so it was only right that he returned the favor.

He wouldn't have had a chance to say much anyway, as right about then Merchant poked her head through the dining room door and, making sure she stayed out of the view of the cameras, motioned for Kevin to come join her in the living room. There was a noticeable look of relief in his eyes as he stood up and walked out.

"The education I got down on the Baja Peninsula was just as valuable as anything I got in a classroom," Maria said. She didn't add, as she absently rubbed at the place where her prosthetic leg met her skin just below the knee, that the cost she'd paid for that particular vacation had been a hell of a lot more than just money.

Mama looked away. "That's not even the biggest problem, honey."

"Then what is?"

"It's just that Kevin is, well…"

"I thought you said you didn't care that he was trans."

"Damn it, Maria, we don't care what's between his legs," Papa said. "What bothers us is that you're sleeping with someone old enough to be, well, old enough to be me."

"Wait, his age? It's his age that's been bothering you this whole time?"

"Of course it's his age," Mama said. "Maria, we know who he is. We know he's kind of famous…"

"More than kind of, Mama."

"But that's not the point. What's going on between you two, it's just not natural."

"What's so unnatural about it?" Maria asked. "It's not even like he's really that old. And he's not old enough to be Papa."

"He's close enough," Papa said.

Felix finally piped in. "Sis, he violates the Creepy Dating Rule. We've talked about this before with your other boyfriends."

"Oh Christ, seriously? How many times do I have to tell you that the Creepy Dating Rule isn't actually a thing?"

It was Mama's turn to be confused. "What's the Creepy Dating Rule?"

"It's nothing," Maria said.

"It's not nothing. It comes from the internet," Felix said.

"So it's nothing," Maria said again.

"Mama, the Creepy Dating Rule says that it's not creepy for someone to date a person younger than you as long as that person is at least half your age plus seven."

"Who made that up?" Mama asked.

"I told you. The internet."

"So, no one," Maria said.

Mama took a moment to do the math in her head. "He violates the rule."

"Told you," Felix said.

Kevin cleared his throat from the doorway. "Um, sorry. I really am. But we need to go, Maria."

"You haven't even had pie yet!" Mama said.

Maria, however, didn't care whether or not she had pie. She was just delighted for the excuse to get the hell out of here. She stood up so fast that she almost tipped her chair over. "We'll take our slices to go."

"Maria, don't do this," Papa said. "Don't run away from this conversation. We've been waiting to have it for some time now."

"It's going to have to wait longer. Sorry, but I'm sure this has to do with stuff for the show. Right?" she asked, turning to Kevin. "Show stuff?"

"Um, right."

"And that's what going to pay for the rest of my education," Maria said, then, because the fact that they had ignored it all night pissed her off, "as well as my medical bills. Learning to walk again didn't fucking pay for itself, you know."

Mama looked more taken aback at her swearing than anything else. Papa, however, looked genuinely hurt. "Now Maria, you know we offered to help. You were the one who…"

"Gotta go," Maria said, storming out of the room. Gary

followed her while Charlene stayed in the dining room to get the reaction of her family. As soon as they were both with Kevin and Merchant in the living room, Merchant motioned for Gary to cut the shot. He turned off his camera and set it down while Maria grabbed her purse from where she'd left it near the front door, clearly ready to leave.

"So?" Maria asked Kevin. "Was I lying? Was it something to do with the show?"

"No, you weren't lying. But don't you want to talk about…"

"No, I don't. Just tell me what's going on so we can get out of here."

"One of Merchant's contacts got a lead on something we can use for the show," Kevin said.

"Wait. Do you mean…?"

"We're finally going back out to sea. That is, assuming you think you're ready."

Maria nodded that she was, trying not to make any outward show of the fact that she wasn't ready at all. She was, in fact, terrified.

3

The miracle of modern television money, even from a relatively small network like TEC, turned what should have been the months-long process leading up to flying internationally into a speedy, well-oiled machine. Both Maria and Kevin carried their passports with them at all times, and given the time they already spent in another country, they were already up to date on all the required vaccinations, ranging from hepatitis to typhoid to yellow fever. Merchant likewise took care of all the travel arrangements as well as fees they would need to pay when they reached their destination, meaning that Maria didn't even have to know exactly where they were going up until they were on a commercial flight to Ecuador. Even then, she still didn't know exactly what they were supposed to do there, nor did she necessarily want to just yet. She'd rather decompress from that rather disastrous family gathering while psyching herself up for her return to the ocean.

The plane ride had been a blessed moment of relief for both of them, as the television crew had gone down to Ecuador on a different flight, giving Maria and Kevin their first real moments of peace ever since Maria had woken up in a hospital in Mexico with her leg gone, amputated after it had been ripped apart by a hammerhead shark. For this ride, they were just a couple again. They weren't world-famous marine biologist Kevin Hoyt. They weren't "the Indiana Jones of the ocean," as one news network had taken to calling her. They were just two people in love with each other.

They slept for most of the flight, taking turns with one's head draped on the other's shoulder. Although Maria woke up with a horrible crick in her neck, she still felt like she'd had her first peaceful sleep in months.

There seemed to be an unspoken agreement between the two of them that they wouldn't discuss why they were going to Ecuador.

Kevin apparently knew, but Maria wanted to hold off on anything that was even remotely related to *Sea Avenger* until she absolutely had no other choice. Months ago, back on the Baja Peninsula and before the Cortez Incident, as the media called it, she'd been the one who'd been all gung-ho about the idea of Kevin having his own reality TV show. Kevin had been reluctant, but he'd liked the idea of being able to bring real marine biology education to the people.

Then Cortez had happened, and Maria's life had been thrown upside down. Now she was the famous one, and while Kevin was still renowned throughout the world, the public had started to act like he was just her sidekick. This was not the life Maria had wanted. But it was either accept the fame and the TV show offer, or else not know how to pay for her medical bills.

There was a limo waiting for them at the airport when they landed in Guayaquil. Kevin, still not saying exactly where they were going, explained that they could have continued by plane to their next destination, but Merchant had thought it would be better for the show if they approached by sea, meaning they needed to get to the docks. The limo wasn't exactly the same as what movie stars might get, but the network had paid a decent chunk of cash to make sure they showed up in style. Once they were inside and the limo was on its way, Maria figured it was finally time to get everything sorted.

"Okay, I suppose we've got to talk about it now. Why are we here?"

"I told you, we're going back out on the sea."

"That I know."

"Are you ready for this?"

"That I don't know."

She hadn't talked about it much, but with Kevin, she never needed to. They'd grown to be able to anticipate each other's wants and needs, as well as their fears. The truth was Maria was scared out of her mind about going back on the water. That was crazy, of course. Being a marine biologist had always been her dream, and a marine biologist that couldn't let herself out onto the ocean was like a circus barker that was afraid of clowns. She'd been in therapy for months now, both to deal with the trauma of the event itself and to get past the constant creeping depression when she remembered that a physical part of her was now gone forever. Her therapist said she was making great strides. Maria wasn't so sure.

"Well, maybe this will help," Kevin said. "What if I told you we're going to fulfill one of your dreams?"

She'd had an idea of where they might be going as soon as she'd seen that their plane was going to Ecuador, but she hadn't wanted to get her hopes up. Now, though, she allowed herself to smile. "Galápagos?"

"Yep." He took her hand and squeezed it. "That's why I knew you wouldn't mind when Merchant suggested it."

She sat back in her seat and thought of the image she'd always had in her mind of the Galápagos Islands. To anyone with even a passing interest in biology, the Galápagos had the closest thing they could picture to a mystical place. The islands of Darwin. The place he had visited during his voyage on the *Beagle*. The land that had started him thinking about the idea of evolution. She'd read *On the Origin of Species* when she was thirteen with the same voracity that other people her age had been reading *Harry Potter*. She even remembered one time geeking out when some of her classmates started talking about *The Voyage of the Beagle*, only to be embarrassed and disappointed when she realized they were actually discussing *The Voyage of the Dawn Treader*.

"Have you ever been there?" Maria asked.

"Once, when I was working on my post-doc," Kevin said.

"Was it amazing?"

Kevin chuckled, then appeared to grow uncomfortable.

"What?" Maria asked.

"Well, yes. It was. But a lot has happened since then. I have colleagues that work there sometimes. They say that it's changed. Be careful about thinking it's some unspoiled paradise."

Despite the warning, Maria couldn't hold back her excitement. She made an audible squee, which made Kevin smile and take her hand.

"There's one thing you need to know, though," he said.

"What's that?"

"We're going to be heading to the islands on the *Cameron*. Merchant was insistent. She says it's just as much a character on the show as we are."

Maria nodded, her expression turning solemn. The last time she had been on the *Cameron*, it had been more or less dead in the water while she lost consciousness and bled out on its deck. She hadn't seen it since the Cortez Incident, and she wasn't sure how she would react when it came time to board it again.

"Alright. We'll deal with that when the time comes." Maria sneered. "I'm sure my reaction will make excellent television."

"Yeah, that's probably what Merchant is hoping."

"So what exactly is going on that TEC wanted us to drop everything and get the first flight to Ecuador? It wasn't anything that could wait?"

Kevin sighed. "Okay. So this is the part where I wish you had let me tell you this earlier."

"I'm letting you tell me now."

"I know that we both wanted to *Sea Avenger* take a more educational angle regarding marine biology, but TEC has been looking for something, anything, that they think would add to ratings."

"Right, not like I didn't already know that. They want us fighting more giant sharks. I've told them over and over that what happened in the Sea of Cortez was an anomaly."

"An anomaly they want to make look common. They want something that can compete against Discovery Channel's Shark Week."

Maria bared her teeth. Kevin knew very well what Maria thought about Discovery's yearly ratings stunt. Once upon a time, it hadn't been so bad. But now it made people have the completely wrong idea about sharks. The final straw for her had been when Discovery had aired a fake documentary that appeared to show that megalodons, enormous prehistoric ancestors of modern sharks, were still alive and killing people. She'd had arguments with people who'd refused to believe the documentary was fake, even after she had shown them statements from the Discovery brass practically admitting to it. That wasn't how Maria wanted to spread her fascination with marine life.

"No. Hell no. I will not participate in anything being faked. I don't care if I have to pay all my medical bills myself."

"Don't worry, hon. That was in the contract, remember? Not even so much as CGI cut scenes. But they want us, and by us I actually mean you, in places that they can make look dangerous. They want you looking like a hero."

Maria took a deep breath. She understood that what had happened in the Sea of Cortez was a one-time thing, that any drama or action that came through in the final show was likely going to be all thanks to editing tricks. But even the thought of being in that kind of situation again made her shiver. True, she had held up under the actual pressure while the events were happening, but that was when she'd still had four limbs. That kind of thing would make anyone squeamish.

"Okay then. So what's the situation?"

"A tourist was killed. They want us to investigate."

"Wait, we're taking advantage of someone's death? That doesn't seem right."

"Trust me, it doesn't sit well with me, either, but the victim's husband has apparently already given his consent for us to be involved. He's shell-shocked and just wants some answers, and the locals don't have the tools or manpower to investigate it further."

"So what exactly happened?"

"Well, um, as far as anyone can tell, something ate her."

Maria blanched.

"Of course, nobody's sure yet. It was a small group of tourists on one of the islands small enough that it barely even merits a name. There were two eye-witnesses, if you can really call it that. The husband didn't see much at all and still isn't talking completely coherently about what happened. And the guide was facing the wrong way. Apparently, whatever happened, it was fast. By the time the guide got a chance to look, all there was left to find was blood and, uh, a few pieces."

"A few pieces?"

"Yeah, um," Kevin looked away from her. Maria realized he was suddenly trying to see anything but her prosthetic leg. "Her arm. All that was left was her arm."

Maria thought about what she knew about Galápagos wildlife. None of the islands, even the largest ones that could actually support a few villages, had ecosystems that allowed for large apex predators. Blood and body parts, though... "Only possibility might be sharks, but none of the species in the Galápagos should be the kind that would attack a human."

"Sharks wouldn't make sense anyway. The woman was on land, a good eight or ten feet above the water. Honestly, I don't think some animal killed her at all. Something else must have happened, and we'll have to be the ones to piece it together. That's why I thought this might be a good one for you to metaphorically dip your feet back in the water with. Seems pretty likely that this woman slipped and fell in the water, maybe killed herself by hitting her head against the rocks, and maybe the arm got caught and ripped off as she fell. I don't know, we'll have to investigate the scene to be sure. We can look into this as best we can, give the husband some closure, and TEC finally has the footage they need for their first episode."

"Still, it feels wrong, taking advantage of someone's death like that."

"I thought you might say that. Which is why I didn't tell Merchant that we were definitely going to do it. If you want, this can just be a vacation. You see the islands of your dreams, the network gets some footage of you testing out that new experimental prosthetic that was made for you, or maybe we get something else suitably marine oriented. Either way, there's still some sea in *Sea Avenger*."

Maria nodded. "I'll think about it, okay? I suppose the least we can do is talk to the husband and the guide."

"Good. Hey, you don't mind that I've been taking point with Merchant for you in all this, do you? I just thought it would be easier if you didn't have to worry about the logistics. You have enough on your plate."

Maria smiled, took his hand, and brought it up to her mouth to kiss it. "That's fine, baby. Thank you. Kind of seems like a step down for you, though, the world famous marine biologist reduced to my manager and sidekick."

"You knew I wasn't comfortable being front and center with the cameras anyway."

They spent the rest of the limo ride snuggling and not talking about anything.

4

Their arrival at the *Cameron* was surreal on so many levels. It would have been strange enough for Maria just seeing the boat again for the first time since the Cortez Incident. The *Cameron* was a converted luxury trimaran, hardly the large research vessel some marine biologists got to work on, but advanced in enough ways to make up for its small size. For a while, the *Cameron* had started to become Maria's home, more so than with her family in San Francisco, more than the tiny apartment she was increasingly neglecting at college, even more than the house Kevin kept on the Baja Peninsula. This was where she had met Kevin, where her love of marine biology had bloomed into deep and everlasting passion.

It was also the place where she had experienced the most traumatic moment of her life. So when she saw it, she was at least partially prepared for the complex mix of longing and deep fear that welled up from down in her soul.

What she wasn't so prepared for was the circus the dock had become in preparation for their arrival. There were five cameras already set up here. Charlene and Gary were among the camera crew, along with a number of faces that were new to her. Merchant was off to one side, looking anxious for the moment when Maria and Kevin left the limo. No one was filming yet, which Maria supposed wasn't much of a surprise. Her first view of the *Cameron* again might have been worthy of a television "Special Moment," but not a shot of her exiting a limo. It didn't fit the image TEC was trying to create for her of a rough and rugged crusader of the oceans.

So they all stood there as Maria and Kevin sat inside the limo, waiting with cameras at strategic angles.

"You ready for this?" Kevin asked.

"I've already been on camera, you know."

"That's not what I meant."

"I know."

"So are you?"

"What happens if I say I'm not?"

"I support whatever you decide to do."

"Even if I decide to go right back to the airport and never set foot on *Cameron* again?"

He paused, but when he answered it was with utmost certainty. "Yes."

Maria nodded. Somehow that one word from him was enough to give her the needed extra strength. "Well, I'm not going to do that. Come on. Let's do our walk of fame."

Kevin smiled. "Remember, you're an action hero now. Walk towards the *Cameron* as though there's an explosion behind you and you're too badass to look at it."

Maria's smile was almost genuine. She would have thought it funny if she still wasn't completely sure about her ability to walk on her prosthetic without stumbling. He hadn't intended for his comment to come across as insensitive, but she couldn't help but feel a little cold inside. It made her wonder if she ever did that to him, accidentally belittling something about him being transgender without realizing it. It was the kind of thing they would need to talk about later when they were alone.

Kevin opened the door and got out first. He waited next to it just to be sure she didn't need help, but she could get out of a car by herself just fine, thank you. Once she was standing, she did her best to give that hyper-competent air the network probably wanted her to show the world.

The cameras were rolling, and she walked toward the dock where the *Cameron* was berthed.

Strangely enough, the boat looked both alien and totally familiar at the same time. Alien in that it had obviously been given some improvements. It had a sleek new black and gray paint job with its name on the side, and there was new equipment on the deck that Maria wasn't even sure she could identify. Familiar though, in that there was no denying that this was the same boat. The boat she had lived in, slept in, and, during one frisky moment at night during a full moon, made love on the deck to her boyfriend. It was also still the place where she had almost died.

Before she could dwell for too long on that cheery thought, a number of people came out onto the deck from the cabin, bringing a genuine smile to her face. One of the cameras turned to watch them as they all gave her enthusiastic applause. Every single one of them was a face she knew. And between them they held a charmingly homemade banner that read "Welcome Back Maria."

The man on the far end, the one who's smile seemed the most forced, was Paulo Gutierrez, the *Cameron*'s pilot. Maria didn't take the forced nature of his smile personally, since it wasn't like he used those muscles any more than he absolutely needed to. Next to him stood Monica Bouleau and the Gutsdorf siblings, Simon and Cindy. All three of them had started out on the *Cameron* as volunteers borrowed from the environmental organization One Planet, but since they had all been present during the Cortez Incident, TEC had decided that they needed to be full-time "cast members." This was a crew she would be happy to work with again.

They might even help her fight back the petrifying fear that threatened to overtake her the closer she got to the *Cameron*.

Action hero. Remember that, she thought, then did her stride to the boat. Walking with the prosthetic leg still felt awkward and alien, but all the practicing she'd been doing up until this point kept her from stumbling too much. The editors would likely cut out any such thing anyway, probably while showing the whole walk in slow motion to make her seem more badass.

The crew came off the boat and met Maria at the edge of the dock. Monica was the first to give her a hug, followed by the Gutsdorfs, while Gutierrez did nothing more than nod at her. Once the reunion had run its course, Merchant ordered for most of the cameras to cut as she approached.

"So you're ready for this?" Merchant asked.

No. I am absolutely not, she thought. "Yes."

"Before we head out, I had something for a possible future episode we need to run past you."

"Whatever happened to this being reality television?" Maria said. "Can't we just once let reality happen instead of trying to manipulate it?"

Merchant glared at her like she was an especially naïve child. Maria supposed she deserved that.

"So what is it?" Maria asked.

"Suzanne Laramie's lawyers have contacted the network. She wants to talk to you, and she wants it on camera."

Kevin and the rest of the crew had already gotten onto the Cameron and were making sure it was ready to set out, but Cindy was still close enough that she heard what Merchant said and stopped to listen. Maria, however, didn't understand.

"Who the hell is Suzanne Laramie?" she asked.

"Right, I forgot how isolated you've been," Merchant said. "Suzanne Laramie is the young woman that you knew better as Diane Mercer."

Oh. Now that was definitely a name Maria remembered. Kind of hard to forget, really, since she was the woman responsible for sinking the *Tetsuo Maru,* an illegal shark-fishing ship in the Sea of Cortez that the *Cameron* had been trying to peacefully stop. All the chaos that ensued after was at least partially Mercer's, or rather Laramie's, fault.

"Is that... is that something that would even be possible?" Maria asked. "By most definitions, she's a terrorist. You'd think the government would have her locked in a hole somewhere."

"I was surprised when I got the invitation as well, but while she's pled guilty to putting that bomb on the *Tetsuo Maru*, she claims she has some other information, something that you and Dr. Hoyt need to know."

"But what information is it?" Cindy asked.

"She said she'll only tell you, Miss Quintero, and only on camera where there's a record of it."

"I'm not so sure that's a good idea," Kevin said.

"And I'm not sure that I'm ready to see her yet," Maria added.

"Well, on behalf of TEC, I have to inform you that the network very much wants this to happen. Could you at least consider it?"

Maria frowned. "I suppose." But she was pretty sure this wasn't something she would change her mind about. There were very few actual human beings that Maria could lay the blame on for the loss of her leg. Laramie was the most convenient scapegoat. While she logically knew that Laramie hadn't had anything to do with the giant hammerhead at El Bajo Seamount or its army of horny shark minions, sometimes logic just wouldn't get in the driver's seat. Maria's purely emotional need was to never see Laramie again and let her rot in a prison cell.

"I'm sure you're up to date on what you're going to be doing in the Galápagos?" Merchant asked her.

"Yeah, but I can't guarantee you that we're going to be able to give this man that lost his wife any answers. Or if we're going to give the network that fascinating hour of television they want."

"Don't worry. You and Kevin just do your thing. Leave it to me and my crew to make something watchable out of it."

Maria tensed. "No lying or making it look like there's something there that's not. We talked about this. It's in the contract."

Merchant frowned. "Miss Quintero, I know we've never talked about your experience with Doug Vandergraf, but I'm fully aware of how unpleasant it was for you. I assure you, I'm not him. I'm not the stereotype of a shady television producer that will do anything at all for ratings. I wish you would let me prove it to you."

"Well, I guess this trip is going to be that chance, isn't it?"

Merchant nodded and boarded the *Cameron*. Everyone was on now, the boat's crew, the television crew, everyone except for Kevin and Maria.

Maria suddenly found herself unable to move.

"Maria?" Kevin asked. "Are you alright?"

Maria couldn't concentrate on his words long enough to give him an answer. This should have been simple. Just step up off the dock, grab the railing for support, and pull herself up onto the *Cameron*. Yet she couldn't. She found herself dwelling, bizarrely, on whether to lead with her prosthetic foot or her real foot. Dimly, she understood it didn't actually matter, but some part of her brain insisted that this decision was of the utmost importance and, if she got it wrong, horrible things would happen.

"Maria, dear, your breathing…"

Still barely hearing him. Come on, she could do this. It was just one step. How many steps did she take every day? How much had she practiced with her new artificial leg? This moment now didn't matter any more than all those other times.

Except it did. Some lizard part of her brain insisted that it did.

"Okay, that's it," Kevin said. "We have to call this off…"

"No!" Maria said. "I… I can do this."

She had to focus. She had to do something, anything, some technique to calm herself down and bring her back into the moment. In that strange way that human brains often have, her mind brought back a song she remembered from her childhood. It was old, and silly, and of course now that she knew marine biology, the logical part of her insisted on telling her that it was completely scientifically inaccurate. Yet somehow, it seemed like an appropriate focus.

"There's a hole, there's a hole, there's a hole at the bottom of the sea," she whispered.

"What was that?" Kevin asked.

"Shh. Give me a moment." She concentrated on the lyrics in her head so that no one else would hear her and think her nuts. *There's a log, there's a log, there's a log in the hole at the bottom of the sea.* Was that how the song went? She couldn't remember, but for now, she didn't think it mattered. All that mattered was that was how it went for her.

There's a bump, there's a bump, there's a bump on the log in the hole at the bottom of the sea.

She felt her mind starting to clear. The gentle sound of the water against the dock and boat became the beat by which she recited the song, and with it went the beat of her heart. She hadn't even realized it was racing until it came back down to something resembling normal.

There's a frog, there's a frog, there's a frog on the bump on the log in the hole at the bottom of the sea.

With her body now feeling under her control her again, Maria lifted her left leg, the real one, up onto the *Cameron*. Finally, she accepted Kevin's help, and he held her hands as she brought the prosthetic right one to join the other.

She looked up at Kevin and smiled. He grinned right back. "I think we're ready," she said. "Let's head off to paradise."

5

The trip would have been much shorter had they come in by plane to one of the two or three airstrips on the islands, but the *Cameron* was just as much a cast member of Sea Avenger as any of the humans aboard, so Merchant had wanted to get footage of them cruising into the archipelago. That meant well over five hundred miles by sea, and more than a single day's trip. The *Cameron* stopped at one point so they could rest for the night, especially considering they'd been going nonstop ever since Merchant had gotten the call that there was something filmable here, and resumed the trip in the morning. That meant that Maria got her first glimpse of the islands of her dreams in the early morning sun, and the view was spectacular.

Her sleep the night before had been restless, partly because of excitement, yet also because she had to once again get used to the gently rocking boat beneath. This meant she was up before the sun and standing out on the deck as it rose. A fine salty mist blew in her face, a sensation she hadn't even remembered that she'd missed until it was back. Standing on the deck was a little harder than she remembered, since she'd only just learned how to balance with her prosthetic leg on the land. The sea took an entirely different combination of muscles. The result was that she actually felt mildly seasick for the first time in her life, but that minor irritation was worth being back in her home element. She had to laugh at herself for how long it had taken her to get on the boat. Now that she was here, she didn't want to leave again.

With the sun at her back as they went westward, Maria's first clue that they islands were almost in front of them were the black specks in the sky. There was some mist that obscured her view, but based on the specks' movements, they were obviously birds of some sort. It had been a while since she'd done much reading on the Galápagos, but if she remembered correctly then this, the month of September, was part of the low season on the islands, a time where, despite their position at the equator, they were cooler and drier. According to Kevin, there wasn't as much to see at this moment in the year—fewer well-known animal-mating rituals, very little in the way of blooming flora- so there wouldn't be as many tourists as other parts of the year.

Maria took out a pair of binoculars and watched the birds as the boat got closer. She could make out just enough to see that they were albatrosses, hunting for food not far from the island. She thought the albatrosses of the Galápagos might be waved albatrosses, but she couldn't tell for sure from this distance. Then, slowly, like it was rising up out of the sea, she saw the first of the Galápagos Islands rising up with the horizon.

"Isla Espanola," Maria whispered to herself. That much she remembered off the top of her head. Not only was it one of the furthest east, but also among the oldest, having been formed millions of years earlier on the same volcanic hotspot that had created the other islands, then moving to the east thanks to plate tectonics, all while being ground down by the wind and waves until it was its current small size. Given enough time, it would wear down until there was nothing left of it above the water, and it would sink below just like countless other islands had before it.

She was so enamored with watching the approaching island that she only barely noticed as the rest of the *Cameron*'s passengers and crew awoke and went about their duties, everything from taking inventory of their supplies to setting up camera equipment. She thought she heard Kevin say something in her ear about breakfast, but she mumbled something in reply that even she was unsure of and he went away, obviously knowing it was better not to bother her. After some time, she realized that Charlene was standing slightly behind her, getting footage of Maria staring out at the island. Somehow, that made it harder for Maria to appreciate the view.

"Dr. Hoyt?" she heard Merchant say from behind her. "Perhaps you could give us a little background about the islands?"

Maria turned to watch him as Gary got into place for the shot. A sound engineer checked Kevin's mike, then, when the engineer gave a thumbs up, Kevin spoke.

"Although it's unknown for sure if anyone might have come here before them, the first recorded people to set foot on the islands was a crew taking the Bishop of Panama to Peru. They ended up off course and found themselves stuck here for a time, where they couldn't find enough fresh water and some of them died. They left thinking that the islands they had found were worthless, little more than a hell on Earth. They didn't even bother to name the islands. The archipelago didn't have a name until years later, when some unknown mapmaker simply labeled them the "Insulae de los Galápagos.""

"Which means…?" Merchant asked.

"Islands of the Saddled Tortoises," Maria said, joining Kevin at his side. Kevin took her hand and squeezed it. She squeezed back.

"After that, the islands were still mostly forgotten and ignored by most people," Kevin continued. "The only people who gave it much thought were pirates and the occasional whalers."

"So what changed?" Merchant asked. "Why did people suddenly start to think they were important?"

Kevin smiled. "What changed was a little ship called the *Beagle*. It was captained by a man named Fitz Roy, but he wasn't the one history would remember as the most famous person on the ship. That person ended up being a young naturalist named Charles Darwin."

This part Maria could jump in on, considering how many times she had read the Galápagos chapters of Darwin's *Voyage of the Beagle*. "When Darwin first saw the islands, his reaction was pretty much like everyone else. A bunch of desolate islands, only a few of which were only close to being useful. He spent five weeks here, and even after he left, he didn't know yet what he had seen. Famously, he didn't even take very good or organized samples of the wildlife here. It was only when he returned to England and started looking at the specimens, along with specimens that had been collected here by other naturalists, that a radical idea started brewing in his mind."

"Evolution?" Merchant asked.

"Sort of. Contrary to what some people believe, evolution wasn't a completely new idea at the time. Some, like Lamarck, had already posited ways such a thing might be possible. But none of that was mainstream. Darwin came up with a specific type of evolution: natural selection."

"Explain it for our viewers," Merchant said. "Maybe we can put some interesting graphics over your words in post."

"The absolute best examples are Darwin's finches," Kevin said. "There are fifteen specific species of finches throughout the Galápagos."

"Really?" Merchant asked. "I thought I saw in my reading that there were only fourteen."

"Maybe in some alternate reality," Kevin said. "But here in our real universe, there are fifteen. The finches are all slightly different in size and coloring, but the most notable difference between them is their beaks. Some have very large beaks, some very small. At some point in the past, a common ancestor to these finches somehow ended up on the islands. There are plenty of different theories as to how, but considering how many different currents converge here, it's hardly surprising that species would end up here. The ancestor finches would have ended up on several different islands, where they would have found different resources at their disposal. One island might have an abundance of small seeds, another of large seeds, another of cactuses, and so on. Even though so many of the islands are close together, the strong currents between them discourage species from going from one to the other. So the various finches are cut off from each other, preventing interbreeding. On the island with large seeds, the finches that would have the best chance of surviving were the ones who could more easily crack open the seeds, meaning the ones with larger beaks. The ones with smaller beaks get less nutrition, and therefore are less likely to survive or mate. If this happens over enough generations, you get a large-beaked finch that is genetically distinct."

"Same goes for smaller seeds," Maria said. "Smaller, easier to open seeds mean the finches that thrive are the ones with smaller beaks shaped for picking up tiny objects. On those islands, the large beak becomes a problem."

"Do that enough times, on enough different islands, with

enough different available resources and enough generations, then viola," Kevin said. "The result is fifteen distinct species of finch where there was originally only one."

"Alright, cut," Merchant said. "I think that's good. I've got to say, though, that I'm not sure how well all that talk about evolution is going to go over at the network."

"Um, isn't the network called The Education Channel?" Maria asked.

"Sure, but it doesn't jive with the opinions of a certain demographic of the American public."

"We're not here to give them an echo chamber about their unfounded opinions," Maria said. "We're here to give them facts."

"Actually, I'm sure the network would say we're here to give them scary things in the ocean," Kevin said.

"Look, I agree with both of you," Merchant said. "I'm just letting you know that I'm going to have to fight to get certain things past them. Too many executives would look at what you were just talking about and would only see a snooze-fest."

"And where do you stand in that?" Maria asked. "Are you really going to fight to make this show everything it should be?"

"I already told you. I'm not Doug Vandergraf."

"That didn't actually answer the question."

"All I can do is show you through my actions, okay?" Merchant said, then turned around and walked away in a manner that clearly told them she thought this conversation was over.

"You're not going to let this conversation be over, are you?" Kevin asked.

"If I have to have my name first in the credits of this show, then I'm going to do everything I can to make it something I'm proud of. You're still with me, right?"

"All the way, honey," Kevin said. They both turned back to look at the islands as more came into view, tall dead volcanoes and round ridges of rock rising up out of the sea. It was gorgeous, and Maria couldn't wait to take her first step on them.

6

The first thing Maria had to do when stepping off the dock in Puerto Ayora was sidestep a pile of animal shit. Under other circumstances, she wouldn't have taken that as a particularly inauspicious sign. She was a biologist, after all, and a major part of biology, whether anyone wanted to admit it out loud or not, was dealing with the leavings of all manner of creatures. It was the size of the turd, though, that gave her pause. It was big. Not quite big enough to belong to a human. More like that of a large dog that had had a healthy lunch. Dogs weren't endemic to the Galápagos Archipelago. They'd been brought here with humans, obviously. Anywhere else, she would have simply walked around dog shit without giving any more thought to it, but here it struck her as an ill omen.

As for an ill omen of what, she had started to feel it the instant the *Cameron* had come close enough to Puerto Ayora to see it from the open sea. She'd had to do a double take, and for an instant, had even thought to wonder if she was even in the Galápagos at all. Because this was not how she had envisioned them.

"I thought you said we weren't coming in at the height of the tourist season," Maria remarked to Kevin.

"We're not."

"But, uh, just look!" She gestured out at the harbor. She had almost expected a sleepy-looking fishing village. Instead, the first thing she saw, before she could even see beyond to the village itself, was a harbor jam-packed full with yachts, cruise ships, and boats of every size in between. Most of the cruise ships had very noticeable logos on them of big-name cruise lines.

"From what I've been able to gather about the way things are around here now, this actually looks worse that it usually would specifically because we are in an off month," Kevin said. "During the height of the tourist season, you're not going to have all these docked at Puerto Ayora at the same time. They'd be spread out throughout the islands, doing their tours. Instead, most of them are taking advantage of the slow time to dock for cleaning and repairs."

"But this is…"

"This is what?"

"This is too many. The Galápagos are supposed to be remote islands separated from the rest of the world and…"

"And frozen in time?"

"I guess. I suppose it sounds naïve when you say it like that. Instead, this is more like a new Disneyland. Wait, is that…?"

Neither of them had commented as the *Cameron* cruised in past a very large cruise ship with a very familiar cartoon mouse painted on the side.

And now that they were walking into the village proper, the picture of a pre-fab resort town only became easier to see. She'd known enough in advance to be aware that Puerto Ayora, situated at the southern end of Isla Santa Cruz, was the largest of a small number of human settlements on the islands. What she'd been expecting was a tiny fishing village. What she got instead might have been a tiny village at some point in the recent past, but now was on its way to something bigger. And, perhaps, gaudier.

There were still plenty of small buildings, but they were dwarfed by the multiple hotels with bright new paint jobs that were obviously run by major hotel chains. The main street was full of souvenir shops, selling everything from stuffed versions of Lonely George, the most famous animal to ever live on the islands, to shirts featuring—yes, it was really true—Disney characters. She noticed a number of small businesses, dingy but well-loved, advertising tours and diving trips. Nearby there were other buildings, much flashier in nature, advertising the same things but also offering stranger and shadier experiences, everything from parasailing to tortoise rides.

"Is that even legal?" Maria asked, pointing to a picture of a child on a saddled tortoise. It was a cartoon, so the tortoise looked inordinately pleased to have someone on top of it. Darwin himself had told of riding a tortoise in *The Voyage of the Beagle*, but she doubted it was something he would have done given their current endangered and protected status.

"Nope. Don't think so," Kevin said.

"So how are they getting away with advertising it?" Maria asked.

"Because they paid off the right people," someone said nearby. Maria, right along with all the cameras that had been following her, turned to see a young man in clean khaki pants and an aloha shirt coming toward them from one of the smaller buildings advertising tours.

Kevin held out his hand. "Are you Ernesto Padilla?" he asked.

"That I am. You must be Kevin Hoyt." He took Kevin's hand and shook it before turning to Maria. "Which must make you the world famous Maria Quintero?"

Maria did her best to hide her grimace from the cameras, instead concentrating on Ernesto. He was younger than her by a couple years and well-built, the body of a man who had grown up doing his share of hard work. He also seemed a little shy and sad as he took Maria's hand. For some reason, that endeared him to her. Merchant had gotten her up to speed on as many details at possible during the hours between mainland Ecuador and the islands, including Ernesto's brief role in tourist Debbie Schmidt's death. He carried himself like he thought he might be to blame for this, and all he wanted was for someone to punish him and get it over with. They would perhaps find out whether some neglect on his part had been to blame, but Maria doubted it. She suspected Ernesto was just being too hard on himself.

"Welcome to the Galápagos," Ernesto said.

"This, uh, it's kind of not what I expected," Maria said. Her vision of the islands had come from her old copies of *The Voyage of the Beagle* and *On the Origin of Species*, long ago read to unrecognizable tatters, and several books of wildlife photography that had captured the Galápagos' pristine nature. Right now, though, all she could see was litter in the streets and an odd, schizophrenic meeting of an old world with a pre-fab new one. Briefly, she almost allowed herself to get excited at the sight of a land iguana basking on the nearby asphalt, but within seconds, it was chased away by a feral cat.

"Yes, well, you could say that the islands are in a transitionary period."

"Most of this wasn't here when I first visited twenty years ago," Kevin said.

"I would have only been a child, but since I didn't live here yet, I can't say whether you are right or wrong," Ernesto said. "Please, let us go to the hotel. That is where Mr. Schmidt is staying. I can answer questions while we wait for him."

This, Maria supposed, was where TEC would edit some stock footage of the islands into the episode while they summarized Ernesto's stories in a more sterilized fashion. Which was unfortunate, because as he talked, Maria couldn't help but feel his passion for this, his adopted home. In the course of only a few minutes, he gave them all a more detailed history of the Galápagos than Kevin and Maria had told on the *Cameron*, starting even before Darwin with the occasional explorer or pirate happening on the islands yet not finding much of use on many of them. Only a few, including the largest island, Isla Isabela, and the one they were currently on, Isla Santa Cruz, had even had sources of water usable by humans. After Darwin had made his journey, there had been others, including captains who'd introduced goats and other invasive species, hoping they would provide food next time ships came through here, but for the most part, the Galápagos Islands had remained fairly remote. Villages popped up, and with them came the fishing industry. And with industry, that was where people seemed to agree that the islands began to change.

"But aren't most of the waters around the islands marine protected zones?" Maria asked him as they sat at a table in a restaurant on the bottom floor of the hotel. The television crew jockeyed for position and scrambled to set things up for their interview with Mr. Schmidt. Ernesto barely even seemed to notice they were there.

"Yes, they are," Ernesto said.

"Then shouldn't there actually not be any commercial fishing in those areas?"

"There is a difference between what should be true and what

actually is," Ernesto said. "It would take a long time for me to go into all the various political arguments and factions running rampant through the islands. To be brief, I'll just say that there are people whose entire livelihood is based on fishing, and they don't take kindly to others saying they can't do it. Sometimes, they get around this legally. Sometimes, corrupt officials make illegal things legal. And other times people just ignore the law completely."

"I told you this wasn't going to be a pristine paradise," Kevin said to Maria with a sigh.

Monica chimed in. "But this is the Galápagos. It's a protected World Heritage Site. Home to unique species that are critically endangered and can't be found anywhere else in the world. Doesn't that mean anything to them?"

"Absolutely. To some of us," Ernesto said. "That's part of the reason I got into the tourist trade. I love it here. I respect it. I want to share that. And I'm not alone. There's a lot of people like me. But there's also a lot of people who see their livelihoods threatened by regulations they don't see the point of. Especially when we've got big companies with giant cruise ships coming in and doing whatever they want because they can afford to pay off the right officials. When people see enough of that, they wonder why they have to obey when foreigners don't."

Maria thought about this while they waited. She could tell that the plain and simple idea of people illegally fishing or hunting endangered species set Kevin's blood to boil. It angered her, as well. But she wondered what it had to be like, living on a tiny set of islands that weren't designed to support humans, watching while the way of life you'd always known was gobbled up by forces around you. As much as she always wanted to put nature first, she could also understand the simple desire to rebel.

Bernard Schmidt came down a few minutes later and, seeing their group at the table, made a beeline for them. Merchant cut him off, though, and said something to him in a low voice that Maria couldn't hear. Although, judging from the perplexed look on his face, she had a guess that Merchant was asking him for a personal "confessional" video before he talked to everyone. She and a camerawoman disappeared with him for about fifteen minutes.

"Ernesto?" Maria asked. "Before we hear Mr. Schmidt's account of what happened, why don't you tell us what you can."

"I would, but there isn't much. Debbie Schmidt was being difficult. She wandered from the path, which I should point out is illegal. When I convinced her to come back and join us, I turned my back for no more than a few seconds. There was a huge splash that knocked me down, and when I got up and turned around, she was gone. Uh, at least most of her was."

"Has there ever been this kind of incident on Isla Niña before?" Kevin asked.

"No, but something you must understand is that up until recently the majority of people weren't even allowed on Isla Niña."

"Why not?" Maria asked.

"All corrupt forces aside, most people do want to do their best in keeping the islands as pristine as is possible in a modern age. That means that, although the primary industry in the Galápagos is tourism now, that tourism is strictly limited. The archipelago consists of fourteen main islands and a number of smaller islets…"

"Wait, I could have sworn there were only thirteen," Maria said.

"Maybe is some alternate reality," Ernesto said. "But here in our real world there are fourteen. Out of all the locations in the archipelago, though, only a small number are open to tourists. The rest are only allowed to have people on them by special permit, usually for scientific or other similar reasons. Up until recently, Isla Niña was one of those sites. When the park opened it up to tourists, only a very small number of permits for it were issued. I was actually quite surprised I got one. I didn't think I had nearly enough money, but I was told that I had qualified for a grant thanks to how long I've been doing this." He sighed. "Now I don't know what will happen. I will very likely lose my permit for Isla Niña, but it might also lead to the park service closing off the island altogether again. There are many people who are not happy about that possibility. Whatever happened out there, Mr. Schmidt and I are not the only ones who want it resolved."

Finally, Schmidt joined them at their table. Perhaps understandably, he struck Maria as a very confused man. He would often trail off, forcing Maria or one of the others to gently coax him back to the topic at hand. Despite Merchant's assurances that he had agreed for them to be here, Schmidt didn't seem to understand who they were or why they were talking to him. Kevin acted as the sensitive one, getting him to talk about his wife and what she had been like before finally getting him to give his account of her disappearance.

"For just that one moment, she almost seemed to be enjoying herself," Schmidt said. "It was a side of her I so seldom saw anymore. And it was all because of crabs. Seriously, crabs. Out of all the things on the island, that's what she found beautiful."

"Mr. Schmidt, I know it's hard, but Mr. Padilla already gave us a clear overview of everything that happened up to the moment where he turned to go back to the trail," Kevin said. "We need to know what you saw next. Everything. Even small details might be important."

Bernie Schmidt paused for a long time before simply saying. "She was just gone."

"But how?"

"Something… look, I didn't see anything, okay? I thought I had, but I didn't."

"I think you did," Maria said.

"Anything I thought I saw didn't make sense, so it can't be right."

"Trust me, we have some experience with things that shouldn't make sense," Maria said. To make her point, she rapped on her prosthetic leg. "Whatever you think you saw, we'll give it a fair shake."

"Anything?" Schmidt asked. "Even if I say it was a sea monster?"

"Is that what you say it was?"

"I don't know. The thing is, it moved fast. Too fast for me to see. All I can say is that it was long. And big. And had a dark color. But the when it came up, there was so much water with it that I couldn't get anything more than an impression."

"And that impression was?" Maria asked.

"The Loch Ness Monster."

Maria and Kevin exchanged a confused glance.

"See? I told you that you wouldn't believe me," Schmidt said. "It's not like I actually think the Loch Ness Monster came all the way to the Galápagos and ate... uh, took my wife. But that's just the image that came to me in the half a second I kind-of sort-of saw it. Then there was a sound, like... like a wet snap. And she was gone, and it, whatever it was, was gone. And all that remained was..."

He gestured at the floor, as though something was lying there in front of him and he couldn't possibly find the words to describe it.

"Seriously, that's all I have," Schmidt asked. "Can I go now? I'm still trying to work through all the, um, arrangements."

"Yes, of course," Kevin said. "Thank you so much for your time, Mr. Schmidt."

Schmidt disappeared back up to his room, allowing the rest of the crew to sit around the table and discuss the case. Gutierrez and Monica had elected to stay back at the *Cameron* and prep for their trip to Isla Niña, while Simon and Cindy had followed them. Both of them had stayed quiet while Schmidt talked, but as soon as he was gone, they became animated.

"Okay, so the first thing we need to do is figure out what kind of genre we're in this time," Simon said.

"Oh dear lord, not this again," Cindy said with a roll of her eyes.

"Excuse me?" Ernesto asked. "I'm not sure I understood."

"That's okay," Kevin said. "It's best if you don't even try."

"Are you two still going on about this?" Maria asked. "I thought you got it out of your systems at El Bajo."

"Are you kidding?" Simon asked. "The way things ended at El Bajo only made me positive that I was right all along."

"Please, help me understand," Ernesto said.

"My idiot brother has gotten it into his head that we're all fictional characters," Cindy said.

"Now, I've never actually said that. I've just implied that maybe we're not real."

Cindy smacked him upside the back of the head.

"Ow, hey! What was that for?"

"That was for saying something stupid. Also, it was a preemptive slap for all the stupid things you're going to say during the whole trip."

"Can we focus for now?" Maria asked. "There'll be time enough for the cameras to catch your antics on our way to Isla Niña."

"So what do you make of what he said?" Ernesto asked, pointedly ignoring Cindy and Simon, instead directing his question at Maria and Kevin.

"Um, I hate to be the one to ask this," Kevin said, "but where are you keeping the, uh, remains that were found?"

"They're at the police station. I don't know if I can get you in to see them, though, if that's what you want. A dead woman is potentially bad for tourism. The authorities have made it clear that they're going to do everything by the book to make sure no American media characterizes them as bumbling buffoons." He looked at Merchant. "Not that you would do that, of course."

"No, of course not," Merchant said. It was difficult to tell if she meant that.

"So we won't be able to get in to see any physical evidence," Kevin said. "I assume that only leaves looking at the actual scene on the island."

"To the best of my knowledge, no one has been back since we left," Ernesto said. "Even without it being currently off limits again, Isla Niña is not a very popular destination. It's mostly without tree cover and only has a few species such as sea lions, marine iguanas, and a number of birds. The people who are most eager to visit are those who know more about what the nature of Galápagos means, not the ones just looking to take selfies with tortoises."

"And you'll come with us?" Maria asked him.

"Of course. Mrs. Schmidt was hardly, uh, a likeable client, but she was a client nonetheless. Whether this all affects my position as a tour guide or not, I want to get to the bottom of her death, if for no other reason than to give Mr. Schmidt some peace."

"We should get moving then," Maria said. "I'm assuming it will take a little bit to get to Isla Niña, and we don't want to waste the daylight."

7

"Maria, are you okay?" Kevin asked.

"I'm fine."

"No, you're not. You're not supposed to be that shade of green."

"Maybe I want to be this shade. You know, just to be different."

"Seriously, what's wrong?"

Maria would have told him if she could, but that would have required her to be able to pinpoint the problem herself. She was standing at the railing near the back of the *Cameron* as it sped north from Isla Santa Cruz, eventually stopping northeast of Isla Santiago, although still well south of Isla Marchena and Isla Genovesa. They had maybe an hour left before they got there. And Maria was experiencing something she thought she'd already gotten out of her system: she was seasick.

"Do you need me to hold your hair back?" Kevin asked. Maria smiled despite the queasy flip-flops of her stomach. Love was sticking by your partner, but true love was still holding them close while they vomited all over you.

"No, I think I'm…" The *Cameron* hit a swell, of which there had been quite a few thanks to the choppy waters characteristic of this season in the Galapagos, causing her stomach to lurch. She leaned over, holding the railing for dear life while she waited for what little food she'd eaten today to come back up. After several seconds where nothing happened, she stood straight again.

This is crazy, she thought. Sea-sickness had never previously been any problem at all for her. It kind of put a damper on the entire concept of marine biology when one couldn't control their own gut, although Maria had had a number of professors who were prone to it but did field work anyway. *Why is this happening to me, though?*

It had to be psychological. That was the only possibility.

Maybe this was some byproduct of the episodes she'd had earlier on the way from the mainland. Or, perhaps, it was that she no longer had her sea legs, both figuratively and literally. She'd been off the waters for too long. She might have been back, but she was only barely able to walk for extended periods of time. Her sense of balance was off even when the floor wasn't shifting and rocking beneath her.

There's a hole, there's a hole, there's a hole at the bottom of the sea.

She didn't have to go any further than the first verse before she started to feel better. "I think I'll be okay now," she said. "Please tell me the cameras didn't catch any of that. It would be embarrassing for the whole world to see the Sea Avenger looking like she's going to barf."

Kevin chuckled. "You're safe. Last I saw, pretty much all the camera people were making a beeline for the Gutsdorfs."

"Oh, this ought to be entertaining," Maria said. Taking Kevin's hand for the extra balance, she went into the bridge, where Gutierrez was making decidedly grumpy noises about the number of people crowding into his space. Charlene and her camera must have gone elsewhere, but Gary and the third camera person, an African-American woman named Lucy, had picked out strategic positions in the cabin and seemed quite happy with the almost vaudevillian performance of Simon and Cindy. Merchant stood just out of camera view, asking questions.

"So what was that you were saying earlier?" Merchant asked Simon.

"What, about genre? We can't figure out what we'll need to do at Isla Niña without knowing what genre our story is in this time."

"Please stop encouraging him," Cindy sighed.

"Look, see, here's the way I figure it," Simon said. "During the last adventure we were on, we faced a giant shark. Now, we never did figure out for certain if we were in some made-for-SyFy movie or if we were in a bad pulp novel..."

"How about neither, you schmuck."

"But it must have had some kind of success, right? Because here we are again. If we go with the idea that we're in a movie, then obviously we're about to face more giant sharks."

"What do you mean, obviously?" Merchant asks.

"The kind of people who watch that stuff aren't very tolerant of innovation, are they? They just want more of the same. But if we go to the idea that this is a pulp novel, then maybe there are more options."

"Simon, there's no way we're going to face a second ridiculously huge sea creature, despite everything that Mr. Schmidt said," Kevin said. "Even just the one was unlikely."

"Exactly! Which is why we have to be in a novel! Because our writer is a talentless hack that can't come up with anything better! But I bet you that he…"

"I told you before, it has to be a she," Cindy said.

"You said you don't believe we're in fiction," Simon responded.

"That's right, I did. But on the ridiculously off chance that we are, I refuse to have been created by a man."

"Uh, that's not how it works, sis. You can't just change a man into a woman because you feel like it. Gender doesn't work that way."

Kevin cleared his throat in a very pointed way. Both Cindy and Simon blushed.

"Sorry," Simon said. "But back to what I'm saying, this is obviously being treated like a mystery. A scientific, vaguely science-fictionish mystery. So here's my prediction about what's going to happen. We'll get to Isla Niña and find a few clues. Then as we're leaving, something exciting will happen."

"I can't believe I'm actually going along with your bullshit," Maria said, "but exciting in what way?"

"Well duh, exciting enough to keep the audience's attention, but not quite a lot yet. That will be saved for the big finale."

"You still haven't explained why we would just happen to run into another giant sea creature," Kevin said. "Other than accusing the author of being a shitty writer."

Simon thought about it for a second, then snapped his fingers. "I've got it! We're not in a book at all. This is a TV show! There's someone or something out there creating sea monsters, and you two are the heroes!"

"Uh, Simon?" Maria said.

"Yes?"

"Do you see the cameras surrounding you? We've already established that we're on a TV show. Just not the kind you're thinking."

This seemed to confuse him, and he wandered away, muttering to himself. "Maybe this is the show-runner's commentary on the nature of reality in the media. If we…" He left the room before Maria could hear anything else, thankfully. His antics were starting to give her a headache.

Feeling comfortable that the show had gotten enough footage of Simon making a fool out of himself that she didn't feel the need to play for the cameras, Maria went below deck and rested in her and Kevin's bed for the rest of the journey. By the time Kevin called down to her that they were almost there, the sun had gone low enough that Merchant kept muttering about the quality of the light. She suggested going back to Isla Santa Cruz and then returning when the light would be better, but Maria and Kevin rejected that. It was already unlikely that they would find any clues as to what had happened to Mrs. Schmidt. They didn't need the wind and water to have even more time to wipe away any evidence.

Maria and Kevin stood on the bridge looking out over the water at the fast-approaching island. Gary stood off to one side, trying to remain unobtrusive while still getting some perfect shot of the two of them. Gutierrez mumbled to himself about the possibility of having to deal with sea lions on the island. Apparently, when working on another boat, he'd once had a bad experience involving a sea lion and a salami, but despite Gary's urging, Gutierrez refused to divulge more, saying simply "some things must never be spoken of in polite company."

Maria only had a vague awareness of this conversation, though. She was too awestruck by the sight of Isla Niña. Judging from her reaction, some might guess that she had never seen an island before, as there was nothing outwardly interesting about the island. Maps had shown that it was roughly circular, the shape of a volcano so old that most of it had been worn away by time so that all that remained was a slightly bulging disk of volcanic rock. The vegetation was little more than a few varieties of grass and cacti. Even the island's name felt inconsequential, as though someone had run out of names and, deciding it was just barely large enough to merit a name at all, had simply called it "Girl Island," and declared the day's work done. An inconsequential land mass, not looking to anyone else like it mattered at all.

And to Maria, it was perfect. After her disillusionment in Puerto Ayora, this felt like the real Galápagos.

"It's beautiful," Maria whispered. Only Kevin seemed to hear, and he squeezed her hand with a smile. In the late afternoon light, she saw birds circling a far section of the island. It was hard to tell from this distance, but their approximate size and shape suggested boobies. Her breath caught in her throat as she wondered if maybe it was mating season, and she might get to watch to delightfully awkward yet strangely beautiful mating dance male boobies used to entice the females. There were no hotels here, no stands selling souvenirs, and few to no invasive species. Isla Niña was the closest she could get to a time capsule back to the islands as they had been when Darwin first came here.

They had to stop the *Cameron* some distance out from the island. There were reefs and volcanic rock outcroppings all over, and nothing bigger than a small boat would be able to land at Isla Niña. Merchant wasn't happy about that because it limited the amount of equipment they could bring onto the island itself. It was eventually decided that Charlene would go with her and Kevin in one Zodiac while Gary accompanied Cindy, Simon, and Ernesto in the other. Monica inflated the Zodiacs while the sound engineer double-checked their mikes.

"You ready for this?" Kevin asked for what felt like the hundredth time on this trip. Maria shrugged and pretended she didn't know what he was talking about, even if she knew quite well. This would be another "first time since" moment—the first time since the Cortez Incident that she had used one of the inflatable rafts. Under any other circumstances, that wouldn't have been a big deal. Except the last time Maria had been in one, it had been thrown into the air from underneath by a giant hammerhead.

Jesus Christ, I can't be scared about everything *in the sea,* Maria thought to herself. *Next you know, I'm going to start being afraid of chandeliers because there were some on the* Titanic.

Getting into the Zodiac didn't require nearly as much mental willpower as when she first got back on the *Cameron*, though, and the brief trip to the island proved uneventful. It wasn't until they tied off their rafts on the rocks that they ran into problems. Ernesto instructed everyone to scrub their shoes, then Gary and Charlene went up the sharp black rocks first. This was followed by a lot of very tricky maneuvers to get the camera equipment up, all so that they could get shots of everyone else climbing onto the island. That seemed like it would be the easy part until it came to Maria's turn and everyone suddenly remembered that she was unpracticed in climbing a rocky cliff, no matter how small it might be, with only one leg. It took her at least three times as long to get up the side as anyone else, partly because she was so out of shape after so much time in the hospital and partially because her prosthetic foot kept getting caught in the rocks. Kevin offered to help her once, but Maria refused in a no-nonsense tone. If she couldn't relearn to climb a few measly rocks by herself, she wasn't going to be able to do any of the real strenuous work out in the field. No one else offered after that.

After many frustrating and embarrassing minutes of trying to climb up, Maria finally made it to the top of the ledge. She took a moment to herself, both to regain some of her strength and to bring her mind back to the situation at hand. Maria took in a deep breath, enjoying the uncorrupted sea air. Uncorrupted, that was, except for the distinct scent of bird shit hanging in the wind, but even that felt right. Large amounts of bird shit meant no humans around to clean it up. Sometimes nature's idea of "pristine" was different than humans.

While they all took a moment to appreciate the peculiar beauty of the mostly barren island around them, Gary listened carefully to something from his earpiece, presumably Merchant giving orders from back on the ship.

"Maria or Kevin, the boss wants one of you to give some kind of inspirational speech about the islands before we leave. It doesn't have to be now. We'll just get the sound and dub it over some of the footage in post," Gary said

Maria waved her hand dismissively. She didn't want to think about any of that TV crap right now. She wanted to enjoy this. As much as one could enjoy an investigation into a woman's death, that was.

"So walk us through this," Maria said to Ernesto. He gave another brief recap of Debbie Schmidt's last known minutes, although unlike at the hotel, he didn't include any of her obnoxious behavior. The woman was dead. No sense dragging something like that out on television.

After that brief overview of where he'd sent everyone, he led them down the path, cautioning them to be careful of a guano-surrounded nest that some booby had built right in the middle. He again cautioned them all to watch their step, not even disturbing any of the plants if they could help it, then took them off the path and to the ledge where Mrs. Schmidt had vanished. Here they all stopped, looking down at the rocks jutting out of the sea water. The arm had been retrieved and was now the property of the Puerto Ayora police, nor was there any more blood. Either animals had eaten it or the splash of waves against the rocks had washed it all away.

"Some of those rocks are pretty jagged," Kevin said. "And slick. It would be easy to believe that someone slipped, fell, hit their head, and then drowned."

"I assure you, there's no way that happened. Mr. Schmidt's story might be distorted by the trauma he's gone through, but at least trust me. This was no simple accident. Out of all the times I've taken tourists out among the islands, I've never let something like that happen," Ernesto said.

"Relax," Maria said. "No one's blaming you." She crouched down closer to the ground, something that was decidedly more uncomfortable than it had once been thanks to the cup of her prosthetic digging into what was left of the flesh below her knee. She needed to get used to it, though. One couldn't be a biologist in the field without getting down on the ground and dirty. "If not for the arm, I could see how this could be interpreted as an accident, though. If the waves hit down there just right, especially if it were at high tide, the spume of water could knock someone off here and into the sea."

"Except it wasn't even high tide," Ernesto said. "It was a little bit lower than now. Look at how the waves are hitting it. We're feeling only a little mist even at the strongest swell."

"So are we honestly considering the idea that a sea monster ate Debbie Schmidt?" Kevin asked.

"You're right," Maria said with a forced smile. "It's highly unlikely. Almost as unlikely as a giant hammerhead that can psychically control other sharks."

"Teddy Bear was not psychic. And that incident is in no way related to this. I'm sure that if we applied logic to this, we could come up with a plausible reason that a woman fell in by herself and somehow lost her arm in the process."

Maria looked up at him from her crouch. "Is this how we're going to do the show, then? You're the one always trying to come up with the logical explanation while I'm trying to prove its more giant sharks?"

Kevin shrugged. "I have no problem being the Scully to your Mulder."

"Except I want to be Scully," Maria said. "Ernesto, you said the tide was lower than this when it all happened?"

"Yes."

"Coming in or going out?"

"Uh, coming in, I think."

"What are you thinking, Maria?" Kevin asked.

Maria tried to ignore Charlene standing nearby, obviously wanting to get a close up as she spouted some important detail to whatever narrative the editors would create of all this. "Let's just ignore the arm for a moment. If she had fallen in or been hit by a wave, wouldn't the tide coming in have kept the body closer to shore?"

"Um, I don't know. Not necessarily. A number of major currents converge on the Galápagos, after all. The way they move between the islands is a major part of why you don't see so much intermingling of species," Kevin said.

"But this close to shore? What I'm saying is there isn't any reason they shouldn't have been able to recover a body. Recovery efforts *were* attempted, right Ernesto?"

"Search boats were called as soon as we could. They didn't find anything beyond, um, what she left behind."

"Okay, so let's ditch the idea that she fell in. It was a bit of a long shot anyway. So what else could it have been, and where's your evidence of that?"

Maria sighed. "I don't have any."

8

Gary and Charlene said they'd been instructed to get "b-roll," which was apparently camera-person-ese for "pretty shots of the environment to stick between editing transitions." Maria was fine with that. It gave her and Kevin a moment to actually enjoy the island before they headed back for the night. They would all stay on the *Cameron* overnight and then come back to Isla Niña at dawn, although Maria wasn't sure what they were supposed to accomplish with that time. This didn't seem like the kind of case that could be solved. Not that she was a detective in the traditional sense (although she preferred to think of all science as detective work), but she knew that when most evidence was washed out to sea and the rest was behind a locked door in a police station miles away, there was little chance of finding any definitive answers. Merchant probably wanted Maria to strap on her specially made prosthetic and jump in the water looking for whatever, if anything, had taken Mrs. Schmidt, but Maria didn't think she was anywhere near ready for that, especially since they still didn't have the slightest clue what the true culprit might be. This was not going to be the action-packed episode Merchant hoped for. All the producer would be able to do was cobble together everything she had so far and hope it wasn't so boring that the show was canceled after the premiere.

She and Kevin found a nearby rock on the edge of the trail where Kevin could sit. Maria chose instead to sprawl out on the ground and, grateful for the chance to escape the chafing so much walking was causing on her stump, unstrapped her prosthetic and let the skin breathe. She refused to look at the twisted snarl of flesh, but it was refreshing to feel that warm island breeze and the tickle of grass. She lay out on her stomach, her chin supported on her fists, as she stared down at the dirt and the microcosm of organisms that lived there.

Kevin, with a pair of binoculars in hand, watched the boobies flying nearby. Maria watched the bugs. To anyone else, that's all they would have been. To her, this tiny sample was just a part of a much bigger chain. Since entomology wasn't her specialty, she couldn't identify the bugs for certain, but she did know enough biology to know these were not the same creatures she would find in her parents' backyard in San Francisco. Some of the ants, maybe, since to the best of her knowledge, ants were not endemic to the islands and all ant species had been introduced by humans that didn't care about upsetting the isolated island's delicate ecosystem. The beetle she watched scurry in front of her, though, she suspected was probably one of the original denizens of Isla Niña, here long before humans had even realized this chain of volcanic rocks existed.

Just sitting here, looking at the beetle and wondering, gave her more joy than she'd had in any other moment since the Cortez Incident. Even her time with Kevin, pleasant and comforting, did not fill her heart in the same way as this simple, tiny show.

"I miss that," Kevin said.

"Miss what?"

"Your smile. I don't see it as often as I used to."

"Hmmm," she said, although it was difficult to keep the expression going now that he had pointed it out. "So, I think that, at least by Merchant's standards, this trip is going to be a bust."

"Big deal," Kevin said. "So instead of the action-packed show she wanted, she's going to get the educational program we wanted. I call that a win."

"Even if no one watches?"

"If something happened to the show, you would still have the money they already gave you. It will cover most of the expenses. If there's any bills left, there's still the book deal you were considering."

"No one's stupid enough to buy a book about me fighting a giant shark," Maria said.

"You might be surprised."

"So level with me. You knew Merchant's attempt at a thrilling first episode was going to be a bust, didn't you?"

"Maybe. As much as Merchant probably would like to think so, we're not going to just run into more giant sharks. Which is exactly why I knew this would be a good way to get you back into the field. No real threat, no real stress, a destination you've always wanted to go to."

"Well, thank you. You're too good to me, you know that, right?"

"I'm exactly as good to you as you deserve. You've been there for me when I've gone through just as bad."

Maria shuddered, thinking back to her early days volunteering with him, back before he'd had his beard, back before he'd been so finely muscled, back when walking into the wrong bar at the wrong time had nearly killed him. They usually didn't talk about that, though, mostly because Kevin didn't seem to want to remember. The mere fact that he would bring it up now, that he would acknowledge it, meant something.

"You know," she said, flipping over to her back and looking over at him with a raised eyebrow, "it's kind of a shame."

"What is?"

"That we're here in paradise, far away from everything, and we've got cameras watching us." She gave him a knowing grin.

He smiled back just as mischievously. "They do seem to be a tad busy at the moment. I'm sure if we found someplace just a little out of the way of eyesight we could get a few minutes to ourselves."

The idea was appealing, but Maria had to laugh as she thought about the possible consequences. "Now Kevin, I'm sure I didn't hear you just suggest violating the conservation rules of a World Heritage Site just to get a little nookie. Besides, we'd probably get unlucky and end up doing each other in a pile of booby shit."

"Okay, this *was* a sexy conversation. Not anymore."

She laughed again. "Granted, I'm sure some shit is sexier than others. Maybe accidentally kneeling in a marine iguana turd wouldn't be so bad. At least nowhere near as bad... as..."

Maria trailed off as something occurred to her.

"Maria, what's...?"

"Shhhh," she said, sitting up and holding a finger up to silence him. Maria listened to the natural sounds of the island. The honks of the boobies. The chirps of finches and other small birds. The occasional faint skitter of iguana's claws on the rocks. The waves as the tide started to come back in.

All the noises she expected to hear on Isla Niña. Except one.

Maria hurriedly strapped her prosthetic back on. "Oh my God. How did we miss it?"

"Miss what?"

Maria tried to stand up by herself and grunted in frustration. She still hadn't mastered the art of standing up from the ground with only one real leg. "Could you help me up, please?"

No longer asking questions, Kevin helped her up and watched silently as she turned in place, taking in the scenery of the island. Mostly flat with the occasional swell of land, rocky and jagged shores, roughly three miles in circumference. As fun as it had been to fantasize about sneaking off somewhere to have sex, there wasn't any practical place to do it. From the right vantage point, as long as it was clear and the light was good, a person could see the entire island from one spot. Anything bigger than a bird would stand out.

And at the moment, the people that had come over on the two Zodiacs were the only large creatures to be seen.

"Scat," Maria said. "We need to search the edges of the island for scat. Any place large and flat enough to act as a breeding ground. A harem."

With those words, Kevin's face showed that he understood where she was going with this, and he was just as amazed that they had missed it as her. They were freaking marine biologists, after all. They should have been paying attention to this sort of thing.

As they both went to the nearest rocky shore and looked for the telltale signs, both Gary and Charlene came up to them, seeing from the sudden franticness of their actions that something must be up. Cindy and Simon had wandered some distance away to whisper whatever brother and sister things they talked about when no one was listening. At the flurry of movement, they slowly made their way back. Ernesto came up to them both, clearly confused.

"What are you two doing?" he asked.

"Help us," Maria said. "We need to find any large piles of scat."

"Scat?" Gary asked.

"Shit," Maria responded. "We're looking for animal shit."

"Then you are not looking hard enough, I think," Ernesto said. "I have seen plenty all over."

"Sure you have," Kevin responded. "Lots of bird droppings, mostly from boobies, some that might be from albatrosses, smaller pockets here or there belonging to finches. Probably find some from iguanas, too. And it's all small."

"I do not understand how that's a problem."

"It's a problem because there should be more. Look around you, Ernesto. Don't you see it? Tell me again, what animals live here?"

"Marine iguanas, birds, sea lions…"

Then he understood.

"We've been sitting on this island looking for anything out of the ordinary that might have shown up," Maria said, "but what's strangest is what we're not seeing. Where are the sea lions?"

They were losing light quickly now, and Maria knew they needed to get back to the *Cameron*. There would be plenty of time to continue their search in the morning. But she already suspected what they would find. Nothing. Nada. A big old goose egg.

On an isolated island in the middle of nowhere, an entire species had vanished without a trace.

Less than half an hour later, they had no choice but to call off their search. Maria had found one area that would have been ideal for a sea lion bull's harem, but it was empty, inhabited now by only a few iguanas and tiny lava lizards. As they walked back to the boats, Charlene prompted Kevin and Maria to explain. "Why is this something significant?" she asked.

"Sea lions don't just disappear. Something happened here," Maria said.

"But, correct me if I'm wrong, aren't there any number of possible explanations for that?"

"Sure, there could be," Kevin said. "Poaching, for one."

"There are many things from Galápagos that are on demand in the black market," Ernesto said. "Sea cucumbers, shark fins, occasionally tortoises. Sea lion penises are believed to be aphrodisiacs in some cultures, so they are on the list."

"Okay, definitely a possibility," Maria said. "But you bring groups out here often, right? Shouldn't you have noticed if someone was out here poaching?"

"Possibly. I don't know."

"They could just have migrated away," Kevin said.

Ernesto shook his head. "Every tour guide on the islands knows that next month is the prime time of year to see sea lion pups. The sea lions should be here, ready to give birth."

"Local extinction, then," Kevin said. "Sad as it might be, that's a very real possibility with most Galápagos species, even without the intervention of humans. The local ecosystem is so specialized, so fragile, that any slight change can cause chaos. During El Nino years, populations of everything on the islands drop."

"Except this isn't an El Nino year, and enough time has passed since the last one that populations should have rebounded by now," Maria said.

"I feel so stupid," Ernesto said. "Now that I think on it, I have not seen any here on the last several trips. The last time I saw one here at all would have been... maybe two and a half months ago? That is what I get for paying too much attention to the tourists and not enough to the islands themselves."

"So what does all this mean?" Charlene asked, pointing her camera right at Maria and Kevin's faces. Maria couldn't give her a good sound bite, though. It probably was poachers. But what if it wasn't? First, the sea lions vanish, then a tourist. What could have possibly happened?

Maria shuddered involuntarily as an image popped unbidden into her brain of a mouth full of sharp teeth coming for her through the crystal blue ocean waters. It wasn't a memory, she thought, not really, just a figment of her imagination. But it was vivid enough that it might as well have been a memory.

"It might not mean anything," Maria said. "But it gives us something to start with." She went back to thinking about the poacher possibility, wondering what they could do to investigate it and how Mrs. Schmidt's death might tie in. It seemed highly unlikely that illegal poachers had anything to do with such a spectacular disappearance, yet she wanted to remain open minded.

The trip back down the ledge to the Zodiacs was easier for all of them, this time. Once they were sure all their equipment was packed up, Kevin took control of the motor of their raft while Simon took the other motor.

"Hey, before we go back, can we cruise around to the site where the woman disappeared?" Gary asked. "We could use some footage of the area from the ocean."

"We'll have to go quickly, though," Charlene said. "We didn't bring anything for night vision with us. It's all back on the *Cameron*."

"Sounds fine," Kevin said. They took the lead, going around the island close enough to the shore for the cameras to get a good shot but keeping enough distance that they didn't rip the rafts open on the rocks. While Charlene concentrated on her shot, Maria leaned over and whispered in Kevin's ear. "We were interrupted earlier, you know."

Kevin chuckled. "Actually, you were the interruptus, my dear."

"We wouldn't have to worry about accidentally lying down in crap in your room, you know."

"You sure you want to do that with so many people on board at the moment? The walls in the *Cameron* aren't exactly thick."

"You never cared about that sort of thing before."

"We never had cameras recording nearby before."

"Uh, Kevin honey? Are you forgetting about that time shortly after I got out of the hospital where we forgot to turn our mikes off when…?"

She stopped.

Kevin laughed. "Maria, if you're afraid about the mikes picking up this conversation now, I think that ship has long since sailed."

Maria couldn't make her voice come out as more than a whisper. "There's something in the water."

Their world went silent except the mutter of the engine and the lap of the water on the sides of the Zodiac. Charlene, having likely heard more of the conversation than she'd been pretending she could, immediately turned the camera in the direction Maria was looking. Kevin slowed the Zodiac down but didn't stop it.

"Where?" Kevin finally asked quietly.

Maria didn't answer. She stared out at the water between the island and the Zodiac, trying to see again what had given her pause. Maybe it had just been her imagination. The lowering light, the movement of the waves, that sense of semi-permanent paranoia that seemed to be a part of her now, all these things combined could have tricked her eyes and mind.

Except there it was again.

"Right there," she said, pointing to a spot on the surface roughly two-thirds of the way from the island to them. The water had churned a little bit more than normal, as though something were moving just far enough beneath the surface that the displaced water could be seen without it showing itself.

"That could be anything," Kevin said.

The second Zodiac came up beside them. "What is it?" Cindy asked. There was an odd tone in her voice, as if she just knew that they were about to see something exciting. Except Kevin was probably right. In a place as teeming with life as the Galápagos, something stirring beneath the water was hardly an amazing occurrence.

Yet Maria's mind wouldn't let it go.

"Just wait. I think."

The surface bubbled and something came up.

Everyone recoiled for a few seconds, then followed Maria and Kevin's cue when they relaxed.

"Just a marine iguana," Kevin said.

Charlene and Gary both got different angles on the lizard as it swam leisurely back to the island. Not something for them to worry about at all, although it was quite a large, wonderful specimen. From its blunt, scaly snout to the tip of its tail, the iguana was probably three feet long, with an impressive fringe along its head and back that, along with the unique protuberances on its nose, made it look something like Godzilla's tiny baby cousin. Maria's heart slowed back to a normal beat.

No, wait, she thought. *Something's still not right*. Galápagos marine iguanas, some of the only known swimming lizards in the world, swam by keeping their legs tight to their sides and squirming through the water much like a snake. It was a form of locomotion that was well-suited to the creatures when they were diving for their dinners of green algae, but entirely impractical at the surface of the water. For the iguana to come to the surface this distance from the shore made no sense.

Unless it was trying to escape a predator.

She saw the shadow beneath the iguana a split second before the water erupted in violence. Maria got the vague impression of something coiling, ready to strike, but the way the fading light reflected on the water kept her from seeing anything else.

Until something huge broke the surface and swallowed the iguana whole.

It moved too fast, disappearing back below the water before Maria could identify more than a dark, slightly beaked mouth so large that the whole length of the iguana fit within the closing maw. The water churned and splashed, rising high enough and with enough force that, despite the distance between it and the Zodiacs, Maria felt the spray on her face. Just as quickly as the mouth had appeared, it disappeared back below the water.

But she could still see the silhouette of something below the surface.

"Holy shit!" Gary screamed. "Holy shit!"

"Did you get it?" Charlene screamed back at him.

"I don't know. I think so."

"Move!" Kevin yelled, trying to be heard above the sudden chatter and panic. "Simon, get your Zodiac back to the *Cameron*!"

"What was that?" Cindy yelled. "Would someone tell me what the fuck that was?"

"Just get away from it! Go, go, go!"

"Gary, keep your camera on where it was!"

"Madre de Dios! Is that… was that… oh hell!"

More panic. More screaming. Everyone moving and shouting orders. A vague sense of leadership starting to develop around

Kevin. The water still moving, whatever had swallowed the lizard still nearby, still lurking, possibly still hungry.

And through it all, Maria didn't move. She didn't even breathe. She couldn't.

She's come for me, Maria thought. *Teddy Bear the hammerhead has come back to finish what she started.* The dim part of her brain still capable of logic tried to say that wasn't possible, that Teddy Bear was far north of here and being tracked. Logic was worthless here, though. Logic wouldn't keep her safe. The shark was coming for her. She had always been coming for her. Teddy Bear had just been waiting for the moment when Maria would forget, when she would be stupid enough to go back to the water and forget that there were things underneath that had tasted her, that wanted more.

Her hands gripped the pliable material of the Zodiac. Her lungs began to burn from lack of oxygen, but she knew that to breathe right now was to die. The water all around her would fill her lungs and she would drown, even as the monsters of the deep ripped her body apart. She had to hold her breath. Had to. Must not…

"Maria?"

The Zodiacs were moving away from the shape under the surface, and although the water continued to bubble with the movement underneath, the unknown thing didn't look like it was following them. That was a trick, Maria knew. Teddy Bear was smart. She could outthink them. All she had to do was wait until the people on the Zodiacs forgot about her, decided she wasn't a threat anymore, and then she would come up from beneath, ripping them, tearing them, shredding them, devouring them…

"Maria, honey?"

Something touched Maria's arm.

Maria screamed. Her fingers, stiffened into talons, lashed out at her attacker, raking against something soft that gave way beneath her fingernails. She'd hurt Teddy Bear. This was her chance. She had to get away. If she stayed where she was, she would be a sitting duck.

"Maria, no! What are you doing?"

The water. She had to get into the open water. Yes, the water was dangerous, the source of everything that wanted to kill her, but Teddy Bear was in the Zodiac now. It wasn't safe. Nowhere was safe. Her only chance now was to get away, far away.

As she tried to crawl over the side of the Zodiac, something got her from behind, circling her, pinning her arms at her side. This was it. She was dead. Teddy Bear was going to eat her. But she would not go down its gullet without kicking and screaming and giving the bitch as much indigestion as possible.

"Maria! Maria, listen to my voice! Listen, Maria."

Her name, over and over. Teddy Bear had learned a new trick? No, that wasn't right. Now the logical part of her brain started to reassert its dominance, reminding her that sharks lacked the vocal cords needed for such a thing. But it still had to be a trick, right? She was still in danger?

"Maria, honey, I'm here. Okay, I'm here."

Shark skin was rough, like sandpaper. Yet the flesh surrounding her was soft, warm compared to the chilly temperatures of the deep. She still couldn't move, which made her fight-or-flight reflex squirm all the more, but the thing holding her was gentle, despite its firmness.

"Maria, you're okay. You're safe."

She was safe? What?

The world started to come back into focus. She saw the light shining on the water, smelled the sea in her nostrils, heard the putter of the motors. Except all of it felt more dull than usual, as though she were sensing everything through a thin gray cloth. There was some distance between then and Isla Niña now, although Maria had not been aware of the passing time. The thing wrapped around her was Kevin, and as he sensed her calming down, he loosened his grip. Now, she could be aware that Charlene had set down her camera in the bottom of the Zodiac so she could work the motor while Kevin held her. Nearby, the other Zodiac zoomed over the water with them, Gary's camera trained right on her face.

"Maria, come back to me," Kevin said. She finally saw his face and the gashes she had left in his cheek when she'd raked him with her nails. "Are you back?"

"Where is it?" she whispered. "Where did it go?"

"It's still back near the island," Kevin said. "Whatever it was, it doesn't look like it followed us."

All she could say was, "Oh." Then, for some reason she didn't understand, she reached down and pulled off her boot and sock.

"What are you doing?" Kevin asked.

She didn't answer because she didn't know. But as soon as her single foot was exposed to the air, she felt like a pressure had left her. Then, as she leaned against Kevin's chest and let a sudden exhaustion overtake her, she began to chant to herself.

"There's a hole, there's a hole, there's a hole at the bottom of the sea. There's a hole, there's a hole, there's a hole, there's a hole..."

9

Kevin had been right earlier. The walls of the *Cameron* were thin. So as Maria hunkered down in her and Kevin's bed, she was still able to hear most of the conversation from the bridge. The fact that everyone was scared and excited probably helped.

"What the hell was all that?" Merchant yelled.

"We don't know," Kevin said. "It was definitely large, and I think—"

"I'm not talking about the thing in the water. Although, Gary, Charlene, please tell me one of you got it on camera."

"I think we both did," Gary said. "Although we'll probably have to slow down the video quite a bit before we can see what it was."

"Good. Very good. But I'm talking about…"

Her voice stopped. Maria could guess that she was probably pointing down in the direction of the bedroom, not that omitting Maria's name made a difference.

Kevin's voice became gruff. "You wanna watch your tone, Mrs. Merchant? That's the woman I love you're talking about."

Maria wished she could force herself to leave the bed and go up to them. If they were going to discuss her, she would prefer that they do it in front of her face, damn it. She couldn't, though. She felt strangely drained and hollow, like that feeling one got after a really hard crying jag, yet without the waterworks. Kevin had given her extra pillows and a blanket, which she had promptly rearranged after he left to form a rough nest around her. The feeling of being surrounding by something soft on all sides, a womb of cotton and synthetic fibers, did wonders to bringing her back down.

"You're right," Merchant said. "I'm sorry. I didn't mean to sound like I might not care. Is she going to be alright?"

"Honestly, I would have needed to see something like that before in order give you an answer. That's the first time she's ever had any kind of episode like that."

"It's just that, with the…" At this point, Merchant's voice evened in tone enough that Maria could no longer hear her through the ceiling. Much of the rest of the conversation turned into nothing but low murmurs, and finally after several minutes of trying to hear, Maria simply fell asleep.

The room didn't have any windows, so she couldn't be sure exactly when she woke up. It was dark, though, and Kevin slept beside her. For several seconds, she felt blissful, her sleep-addled mind sure that they must have fallen asleep together after making love. Then she remembered everything that had happened before. She turned over on her back and stared up at the darkened ceiling, trying her hardest not to think of anything at all.

The change in Kevin's breathing gave her the first hint that he was awake, but she didn't dare say anything. With luck, he wouldn't realize that she was awake too and try to talk to her, eventually just going back to sleep himself. She didn't know if she was ready.

He didn't talk. Kevin just put an open hand on her chest. After several moments, Maria grabbed it, clenching it close to her heart. And they lay that way for quite some time.

"They think I'm crazy," Maria finally said.

"They don't think you're crazy."

"Yeah? Well, *I* think I'm crazy."

"I heard once that if you can tell that you might be crazy, then you aren't crazy because crazy people can't tell that they're crazy."

"I don't think that's actually a thing."

"No, I suppose not."

"Stick to biology. Psychology doesn't suit you."

They were quiet for a few seconds before he said again, "You're not crazy."

"Look, I'm obviously not well, okay? I mean, I tried to jump out of the Zodiac into the middle of the open ocean."

"I admit that no one thinks that's a sign of perfect mental health. But come on. I'd be more worried if you weren't showing strains of hurting after everything you've been through. Craziness isn't the word you should be using."

"Then what word should I use?"

"I don't know. Working through things? Occasionally requiring a mental break from reality? Almost anything is better than using a word with so much negative stigma."

"You sound like you're doing one of your scientific lectures, but with much more of the pulling crap out of your ass."

"Is it working?"

"I don't know." She sat up in bed and looked down at herself. She was still in all her clothes, which were stiff from the salt of seawater. Her prosthetic was abandoned at the edge of her bed. She also had no idea where her boot or sock currently resided. Jesus, what had that part even been about?

"I don't like this," Maria said.

"I know."

"It's not how I think of myself. Maria Quintero doesn't freak out under pressure."

Kevin didn't speak, although his silence said everything. Apparently, now, Maria *was* the kind who cracked under pressure. Was this something she would be able to overcome, or was that simply a new part of her reality?

It wasn't something she could approach from a purely scientific direction, so instead it was time to turn her attention to something that *could* be analyzed and quantified. "That thing that was in the water. We need to figure out what it was."

"Maria, are you sure you're ready to start working this problem?"

"No, but I *am* ready to stop not working on a problem at all. Come on, work with me. I need this."

"Okay." Kevin got out of bed and retrieved his clothes. Maria might have fallen asleep fully dressed, but he'd been in nothing but his underwear. For a moment, Maria wanted to grab him and pull him back into bed where they could forget about this whole thing for a time, but she wasn't sure that would do her much good. After a brief time of pleasure, she would be right back to staring at the ceiling and wondering what the hell was wrong with her.

"So tell me what you've figured out so far," Maria said as she struggled to put her prosthetic back on.

"Not a whole lot. It was decided that we would go over everything we knew and had in the morning, when everyone had rested and was refreshed. We all had a rather hectic day yesterday."

Maria's cheeks grew hot, knowing that she was the cause of much of the problems.

"But you must have discussed something during that whole time. I even heard some of it."

Kevin paused in pulling his shirt over his head. "You did?"

"Yeah. Some of it near the beginning."

"I'm sorry you had to hear any of that."

"Let's not talk about that. Let's discuss our mystery creature, okay?"

"Not much to discuss yet, but maybe the Gutsdorfs have something for us by now."

"You've had them working on it all night? Are you sure that's a good idea?"

"Hey now. Cindy has a perfectly level head on her shoulders."

"And her brother?"

"Her brother is, uh, good-looking? I don't know, that's the best I can think of right now."

"Actually, I'm sure he'd appreciate it."

Maria hadn't given much thought to where they were at the moment, but when they came out on deck, she saw that the *Cameron* had come back in to Puerto Ayora while she'd been sleeping. Gutierrez, despite having his own perfectly fine bunk below deck, was sleeping on the floor of the bridge. Monica was on the deck doing routine maintenance on the Zodiacs. When Maria came out, Monica smiled and looked like she wanted to say something, yet Maria couldn't help but see a noticeable hesitancy, as though she were afraid she might damage Maria if she got too close.

"I'm not going to break, you know," Maria said to her, possibly with more contempt in her voice than she had intended.

"Huh?" Monica asked.

Oh. Maybe Maria hadn't seen her hesitate at all. She quickly got off the *Cameron* before she could embarrass herself further. Kevin stayed behind long enough to whisper something to Monica before joining her.

"What did you say to her?" Maria asked when they were both off the docks.

"I just told her to be patient with you."

"People shouldn't have to be patient with me."

Okay, she was getting irritable now, and this was not how she wanted to spend this fine day in paradise. From the sun, she had to guess it was mid-morning, so she had probably slept for nearly twelve hours. She never slept that long, but after the moment she'd had in the Zodiac, she had felt strangely drained.

"So where are we going?" Maria asked.

"Merchant has set up a sort of base-camp for her crew in one of the for-rent bungalows. We'll go there and touch base with her, and also see whatever there is to see in the videos from last night."

"Uh, what all did they get on camera?"

Kevin gave her a bemused look. "Not enough of what we need, and probably more than what you would want."

Crap. Okay, fine. She would deal with that soon enough. "Okay, then what?"

"Then, assuming Merchant was able to pull the strings she said she could with the American embassy in Ecuador, you and I will be off to the police station to examine the remains, or I guess it's just 'remain,' of Mrs. Schmidt."

"Wait, we're going to be able to do that?"

"Yeah, we've all tried to keep what we saw last night quiet, but it wouldn't surprise me if rumors have started to get around that there might be something out at Isla Niña. When we came in last night, suddenly the police were a whole lot more cooperative."

Indeed, as they walked through the streets of the village, a large number of the locals were giving them stares somewhere between suspicion, anger, and awe. "Where's Ernesto?" Maria asked. "He might be able to give us a better idea of what the residents are saying."

"Last I saw him, he went back to his home, but I invited him to join us later. I thought maybe he might help give us some context as we examine Mrs. Schmidt."

The people they passed on the street had a strangely subdued manner, despite the clear and perfect day. It was as though they were expecting a storm to come in at any minute. A short man in a white dress shirt and a too-tight tie saw them and made a beeline for Maria. Even before he opened his mouth, the way he stood and presented himself alone was enough for Maria to label him as some form of politician.

"Ms. Quintero?" the man asked. "Ms. Hoyt? Susanne Merchant said I might be able to find you this morning. I'm sorry that I didn't have a chance yesterday to greet you both on your arrival." He held out his hand to Maria. There was an awkward moment where she didn't take it, not just because something about the man exuded the stereotypical sliminess she associated with any bureaucrat, but also because whether he knew it or not he had just deeply insulted her boyfriend.

"Mister," Kevin said.

"I am sorry? I do not understand," the man asked.

"My name is Mr. Kevin Hoyt."

Maria gave Kevin a quick glance in an attempt to read his emotions. Kevin had been taking hormone treatments for long enough that it was rare that anyone read him as anything other than a cisgender man. It was possible that this man had made a mistake in his English, but the only other option was he'd known well in advance that Kevin was transgender and had made the slight on purpose.

"Yes, well..." The man withdrew his hand from Maria. Not only did he not offer it to Kevin, he continued to look only at Maria as though she were the only one here. "My name is Mario Estevez. I am the mayor of Puerto Ayora." The way he said it implied that he was sure that Maria must surely already know his name well. She didn't, although out of the corner of her eye, she saw Kevin tense up. He knew that name, and it apparently didn't give him warm fuzzy feelings.

"Mister mayor, it's a pleasure to meet you," Maria said, even though she already had a feeling it wouldn't be.

"Mrs. Merchant has already spoken to me about the needs of

your production, and I wanted to let you know personally that you will have my support."

"Um, thank you."

"Do you have any thoughts on when you and your people might be leaving?"

Oh yeah, Maria thought. *Very welcoming.* "I can't say that I know that for sure. Merchant would know better."

"Yes. I see, I see. Then perhaps you might be able to tell me when certain authorities might be lifting the ban on travel to Isla Niña?"

"Uh, I actually don't know anything about that," Maria said before turning to Kevin. "There's a ban?"

"There was already one in place before yesterday, but what little communication I had with the park service employees and the officials in the Ecuadorian Navy suggested it would stay until we could figure out what was out there."

"If there's really anything out of the ordinary at the island at all," Estevez said. "There has still not been any proof provided to me."

Oh, there's proof, Maria thought, but didn't say it. If no one had told them what they had caught on film yesterday evening, then they probably had a good reason for it.

"I'm sure we'll be able to give you something soon enough," Maria said.

"Good, good," Estevez said. He stood there for a second, staring at them both, as though waiting for a cue. When Maria didn't provide it, Estevez cleared his throat.

"So how much?" he asked.

Maria blinked. "Excuse me?"

"How much? How much money must I give you to declare Isla Niña safe and then go away?"

"Are… are you trying to bribe us?"

"Your presence here is disrupting, but it is September. A slow time of the year. Come next month, though, I cannot have one of the Galápagos' attractions closed to the public."

"You do remember that a woman died, right?" Maria asked. "Don't you want to get to the bottom of this?"

"I don't want people to die, no, but reports of a sea monster at one of the islands…"

"No one said it was a sea monster," Kevin said. Estevez waved a dismissive hand at him, much like Kevin was a mosquito that was in danger of getting slapped.

"Everyone is saying it is a sea monster. They were saying that before you came, but most people didn't take it seriously. But when your group came back so quickly last night, and obviously agitated, it did not matter what anyone said. The rumors are spreading. Citizens are getting anxious. And anxious citizens make poor tour guides."

"And if there is something out there?" Maria asked. "Something that could hurt more people?"

"There isn't. There are just lizards and birds that idiot tourists will pay big money to take their picture. That's all that's ever been on these islands. So please. I say again, how much?"

"You know, there might just be one or two situations in life where I could be bribed," Maria said, "but this wouldn't be one of them."

"It took me a long time to convince the park people to open up another island to the public. I will not have that effort sabotaged by a couple of Americans that have no idea what it means to be a Galapagueno."

"Is that supposed to be some kind of threat?" Maria asked.

"No threats. But I have friends. I can make things happen. If you work with me, you can benefit as well."

Estevez turned and walked away without any goodbye.

"You know, sometimes I do wonder if Simon is right about us being in fiction," Kevin said.

"Why do you say that?" Maria asked.

"Because that? That right there? That was such a cliché. The officious local politician who refuses to heed anyone's warning. This is always followed by mayhem."

"You looked like you knew his name," Maria said as they continued toward the bungalow.

"Yep, I did," Kevin said. "I have word from a contact of mine that several environmentalist groups currently have a lawsuit against him."

Maria snorted. "Of course you have a contact. You always have a contact. Simon would say it's a plot device to tell me information I need for the story. What's the lawsuit about?"

"He did a very public stunt where he took an ax to a number of rare protected mangrove trees near his office."

"Why the hell would he do that?" Maria asked. Anyone else might have wondered what the big deal was. Maria, however, knew that mangroves growing near shores provided important, specialized habitats for certain marine communities. In the Galápagos, destroying mangroves might as well have been the same as slaughtering a group of endangered animals.

"He claims he didn't. He said he was just removing dead branches, despite the video on YouTube where you can clearly see he's hacking apart very living vegetation. In case you couldn't guess from the way he was acting, he has a tendency to put economics ahead of the environment."

"Uh, this is the Galápagos Islands. Aren't their environment and economics the same thing? No rare animals and habitats, no tourist trade."

"See, you're thinking with a long view. I don't think that prick can think any farther than his wallet."

Maria stopped on the sidewalk, letting a number of tourists pass her by. Kevin kept walking for a few steps before he realized she was no longer at his side. "There a problem?" he asked.

"I'm sorry," Maria asked. "Are you okay?"

For just a split second, she could see that he was not okay, but he immediately put up a mask to cover it. "I don't know what you're talking about."

Maria kept her voice soft, gentle, a sign that she wouldn't pry but wouldn't ignore this either. "Yes, you do."

"It's nothing. Don't make a big deal out of it."

"Kevin."

Kevin looked around them at the tourists, many of whom were now openly staring at them. He took her arm and pulled in between a café and yet another building advertising tours. "Okay," he said, his voice so low Maria almost couldn't hear him. "It bothered me. But it's not a big deal. Really."

Maria wondered for a moment if she should push it. She was just about to decide that if he didn't want to talk about it then she would let it slide, then he spoke again.

"It's just... It's been years. It shouldn't bother me anymore, should it?"

Maria didn't say anything. She figured this was the kind of situation where she could do the most by doing nothing but listening.

"One word. One God-damned word. It shouldn't hurt. It shouldn't drive a knife into my gut and twist it. It shouldn't make me want to grab a bottle of Jack Daniels and down the whole thing. I'm supposed to be stronger than that. And yet, apparently I'm not. And no one else gets it. No one else understands just how badly a single word can hit you."

Maria could see the tears forming at the edges of his eyes. She took his hands and squeezed them gently, yet still kept quiet.

"Not 'miss.' Mister. Is that really so hard?"

Maria wanted to speak, wanted to tell him that Estevez was a piece of crap whose opinion didn't matter. But she'd had more than enough people try to say reassuring things to her during her recovery, not realizing that their attempts only made it worse, only emphasized to her that she was different now, that she would never be the same.

Kevin had never done that. He'd just sat by her side and been her silent rock. So she followed suit, doing nothing more than touching him and letting him know that she was there. After Kevin took a few deep breaths, he nodded as though telling himself that he'd gotten past Estevez's little insult.

"Okay," he said. "Let's go see if we can find a sea monster, huh?"

10

The bungalow, like so much in Puerto Ayora, was a weird mix of traditional fishing village and modern tourist. The building itself was probably about thirty years old, but sometime recently, it had been painted a bright, obnoxious green. A pair of iguanas, these ones of the land variety and much smaller than the one they had seen in the water last night, sat in front of the door in mid-copulation. Kevin gently shooed them away before knocking and entering. Inside, much of the furniture had been moved around so that Merchant and her people could use it as a makeshift studio. In one corner, a chair had been set up with a camera and lighting in front of it. Maria sighed. She knew what that meant. A "confessional." The place where she or Kevin would be expected to sit and explain what was going on to the audience at home. Including, most likely, what had happened to Maria last night.

Merchant was off in a far corner on her cell, pausing only long enough in her hushed conversation to look in Maria and Kevin's direction. One of Merchant's crew, a young man named Ted Shirr, brought them both coffee and hooked up their mikes for the day. While this was going on, Maria and Kevin stood behind Gary and Charlene, who had a laptop set up on a folding table in front of them as they went over the footage they had taken the day before.

"Okay, so we've done everything we can to get a clear picture," Charlene said, "but this isn't the movies, and we don't have access to all the state of the art equipment. Maybe we can analyze the footage a little better when we get back Stateside, if you still think we need to."

Kevin looked at Maria. "Are you ready to see this?"

"Don't look at me. You're the one with a Ph.D. You're the one who's going to do most of the identifying, assuming we can."

"That's not what I meant."

"I know that's not what you meant. I was deflecting. Do try to keep up, dear."

"Wait, don't start watching the video yet," Gary said. "I need to make sure we get good shots of you watching and talking about it."

Maria tapped her foot impatiently as Gary and Ted finished their prep. Or she tried to. She forgot that she was balancing on one fake leg, and the attempted motion almost made her lose balance. Kevin grabbed her shoulder, both calming her and steadying her.

"Okay, all set," Gary said.

"So here's what we got, starting with normal speed," Charlene said, starting up the video on the computer. "This was camera one." Gary's camera. The video started at a point where he was pointing that camera back at Isla Niña, a shot that all by itself would have been beautiful. Then there was the sound of multiple people murmuring, and the camera turned in the direction of the ruckus to show the marine iguana coming to the surface before swimming back to land.

"And here we go," Charlene said. The water beneath the iguana became pure churning violence, and something huge came up from underneath, snapped shut over the iguana, and vanished.

"Shit," Maria said.

"Language," Kevin muttered to her. "Remember we're being recorded."

"Shit," she defiantly said again. "I don't remember it happening so fast." She looked to Kevin. "Were you able to see anything useful?"

"Not sure," Kevin said. "Can you make that part of the video bigger and slow it down."

"Yes to both, but making it bigger won't make it any clearer. We've already tried. Hold on."

Charlene did as he said, but she was right. It didn't give them a much better view. "We might be able to do more with the image when we get back to the mainland."

"I'm not sure that we want to leave long enough to do that, though," Kevin said. "The Galapaguenos already seem to be on edge."

"Or at least the mayor," Maria said. "Hey, maybe you guys

could run over and do an interview with him? The more you annoy him, the more I'll try to get you a bonus on your next check."

"What do you think the locals would do, though?" Ted asked as he handed both Kevin and Maria their coffees. "The island is already off limits again. Just keep it that way while you head back and get any new info you might need."

"Not that easy," Kevin said. "I know somebody in Sea Sheppard who has spent some time in the Galápagos." He nodded at Maria. "That's the contact I was talking about earlier. He's how I knew that things here weren't exactly the perfect paradise you imagined."

"I thought you weren't a fan of Sea Sheppard?" Maria asked.

Kevin shrugged. "I'm not. But I knew Danny before he joined them. He's a good man, whether I agree with the organization's methods or not."

Maria let that part drop. He'd made his feelings on Sea Sheppard evident in the past. Sea Sheppard was a group self-appointed protectors of the ocean's inhabitants. They always seemed to operate within the confines of the law, but only just. They'd been known to sink whaling ships, but since they only did it when they were in port and had no crew, and because whaling was supposed to be illegal, they technically weren't doing anything wrong according to the law. As an organization, they'd become more famous recently because of, of course, a reality show. Kevin tended to think of them as being more reckless than needed. Maria gave them a little more benefit of the doubt.

"Anyway," Kevin said. "Any laws regarding illegal fishing or poaching are supposed to be enforced by the Ecuadorian Navy. Except they don't enforce much at all. There's lots of rumors of money handed under the table for them to look the other way, probably some from the mayor himself, although Danny hasn't found any concrete proof. So any attempt to keep people away from Isla Niña would be incredibly difficult. Sea Sheppard used to contract with the Charles Darwin Research Station and Galápagos National Park to patrol, but they've been held back by both interference from the Navy and a lack of funds."

"So you mean to tell me that, in a World Heritage Protected Site, one that is of the utmost importance to biological research and contains large numbers of critically endangered species, no one is trying to protect any of it?" Maria asked.

"I didn't say no one. It's just that the number of people trying to exploit it is far larger."

"So what does that mean for Isla Niña?" Ted asked them.

"It means that the quarantine of the island is pretty much in name only. It means we can't leave until we have a better idea of what's out there. If that thing's endangered, people might try to take it or kill it for their own financial gain," Kevin said. "And if it's dangerous, other people besides Mrs. Schmidt might die."

"Is that the hypothesis we're working with, then?" Maria asked. "Whatever this thing is, that's what killed Debbie Schmidt?"

Kevin leaned closer to look at the paused image on the screen. "It certainly looks big enough. And we already know that it's carnivorous."

"That doesn't mean anything," Maria said. "Whale sharks are huge and carnivorous, but they don't eat anything much bigger than krill. There's no proof yet that this thing looks at a human as lunch."

And yet, she realized, she didn't want to get anywhere near it. The higher part of her brain might have been going back into biologist mode, yet the thought of boarding the *Cameron* again and getting anywhere near it scared the piss out of her.

Merchant finally came over and joined them. "So what do we have? Do we have another sea monster or not?"

"Please don't call it that," Kevin said.

"You just called it that before we got here," Maria said.

"Yeah, between you and me. But we've already got too many rumors floating around, and a questionable politician poking into it. Whatever this thing is, it's some kind of animal. If we, the people who are supposed to be experts, call it a monster, and if that gets around, then the Galapaguenos will be in even more of a panic than they were before."

"Whatever," Merchant said with an uncharacteristic sound of

defeat in her voice. "Where did the Gutsdorfs go?"

Maria suddenly realized that she hadn't seen them since they got here. "That's a good question."

"They left right after you started your call," Gary said. "Don't know where, although I think Cindy said something about wanted to visit the Charles Darwin Research Station."

"Doesn't matter, I guess. We've got enough comedic relief for now."

"What's wrong?" Kevin asked Merchant. "I would think you'd be overjoyed by this turn of events."

"Just because this is going to make good television doesn't mean I'm happy about the possibility that there's something out there eating people. Give me some credit. But also, I just got off the phone with TEC's lawyers."

Maria tensed. "What did we do?"

"None of us did anything. But you don't need to think about confronting Suzanne Laramie anymore, Miss Quintero."

"Why? Did whatever plea deal she was working on fall through?"

"No. She was found dead in her cell three hours ago. Laramie killed herself."

11

Both Maria and Kevin did everything they could to remain polite and courteous at the police station. Ernesto met them there, although he couldn't stay. He, unfortunately, had to deal with mounds of insurance paperwork regarding Mrs. Schmidt. His brief appearance seemed to calm the locals. Still, the police had plenty of reasons to distrust outsiders throwing around their muscles, and the last thing either of Maria or Kevin wanted was to give the residents more reasons to be distrustful. Some of the officers let them into the morgue with wary eyes, but the coroner himself shook their hands happily and welcomed them in. He didn't speak more than a little English. Kevin knew some, but Maria was fluent, so she acted as the translator between him and Kevin.

"The way he's acting, you would think this is a party and we're the guests of honor."

"Actually, it's you that the guest of honor," Maria said. "He's familiar with your work. Says he even worked with you a little bit as a volunteer when you were here once long ago."

Kevin stared at him for a long time before smiling. "The teenage boy with the pink bucket, right?"

Maria translated for the coroner, but she didn't need to translate his response back. The pure joy that someone like Kevin remembered him was palpable.

Maria was ashamed to admit that she had expected the morgue to be little more than a refrigerator and a couple of cots. She should have known better than to assume that just because they were in a small village far from the mainland that meant law enforcement couldn't be professional. Instead, the morgue was small but clean and tidy, the coroner obviously running a very tight and professional ship here. Mrs. Schmidt's remains, however, were in fact being kept in an evidence bag in a refrigerator. The coroner explained to her that there hadn't been much point in using one of the normal body drawers for just one arm.

As Kevin and Maria put on masks and gloves, and the coroner retrieved the arm and prepped if for their examination, Maria's mind wandered back to what Merchant had said. Suzanne Laramie. Dead. It shouldn't have been something that affected Maria, and yet it did. The young woman had been responsible for many deaths, even if she hadn't intended for that to happen. She had, however, set events in motion that had led to Maria being permanently maimed, and Maria saw no reason to forgive her for that. But this fate just seemed too harsh. She'd been found hanging from the bars of her cell with a makeshift noose made from her bed sheets around her neck. Reportedly, no one had had any clue that the young woman was even suicidal, although Maria understood how she could get that way. Not only were the deaths of so many people from the *Tetsuo Maru* on her hands, but there had also been her boyfriend, ripped apart in Teddy Bear's jaws while Diane, or rather Suzanne, had been right there next to them. Maria had her own inkling of what that kind of trauma could do to a person's mind.

And yet, something felt strange about this. Why would Laramie have killed herself if she had wanted to say something to Maria? Maria had thought that maybe the woman had left a note for her, but Laramie's lawyers said there was nothing.

Maria thought again, although mercifully briefly, of the events in the Sea of Cortez over El Bajo. Laramie and her boyfriend Murphy (it suddenly occurred to Maria that she couldn't even remember his real name) had been working with someone else. That someone or someones had made an attempt to kill her before. Maybe they had done it again, and this time succeeded.

That was definitely something Maria wanted to follow up on when they got back to the US, but right now she needed to concentrate on Debbie Schmidt, or at least all that were left of her. Gary had followed them and seemed to be debating whether or not he should film a stiff, bloody severed arm, then shrugged and started recording. If they couldn't show it on TEC, the censors could always blur it out later.

A boom mike operator stood nearby, holding the mike over the coroner's head. To his credit, he was able to ignore the television equipment and maintain a completely professional demeanor. He set the tray holding the arm on a stainless steel table in front of them, explaining to Maria what he had been able to find out so far.

"As far as he can tell, the arm was definitely bitten off, or at the very least wasn't ripped off when it caught on something like we might have theorized. The wound is too even for that. In fact..." Maria frowned at the coroner and asked him a question in Spanish. The coroner shrugged and gave a short response.

"What did he say?" Kevin asked. "I only got some of that."

"He says the wound is almost too perfect. Like, if it wasn't for the circumstances, his first guess would have been to say that someone had cut it off, maybe with a pair of strong but dull scissors."

"Hmmm," Kevin said, then gestured for her to get closer. "This is your show. You want to take point on this?"

"Uh, you're probably better at the lab work than I'll ever be. Be my guest." While she knew that was true, in actuality, she didn't want to get near the thing. The coroner had done a good job preserving the arm for this long, but it was still a severed body part. It gave off the slightest hint of a rotting meat smell, and flecks of blood that had dried around the wound were sloughing off and making Maria queasy.

And, if she thought about it too much, it made her think of other missing body pieces. Her leg began to itch at the shin, her right one, the one that wasn't actually there. She really, really needed to scratch it. Also, she was getting that same weird urge again that she had in the boat, that her left foot needed to be let out of its boot immediately to breathe.

There's a hole, she thought to herself. That single assertion helped to calm her mind enough to observe.

"To start with, let's see if we can get any kind of sample off it," Kevin said. "Not likely, considering how soaked it got from the splash of water, but we should try."

Maria conveyed his request to the coroner. She was surprised that he had a swab and the tools to try to get a DNA sample, but not so much by what he told her next. "He has the means to take samples thanks to some borrowed tools from the Charles Darwin Research Station, but he says there's nowhere on the island that could analyze them. Still, we can take whatever we find to the CDRS, and they can fly the sample out on their next supply flight. If Merchant pulls some more of her strings, maybe we can get the analysis bumped up and have the result in a few days."

"A few days," Kevin muttered. "Do you think we have that long?"

Maria shrugged. "Do we really have any reason to think we can't keep things under control for a few days?"

"You do realize that if Simon were here, he'd point out that, according to the rules of a monster movie, you've just guaranteed that something bad is going to happen very soon?"

"Yes, but sometimes I don't think Simon is all there. Who knows what he would be like if he didn't have his sister around to knock some sense into him."

They took as many samples as they could with what they had, taking extra care to get anything they could from the wound itself. If the arm had in fact been bitten off, then that would be the most likely place to find the DNA of whatever had done this. Kevin's task was to make a closer inspection of the wound itself, looking for bite marks.

"He's right about the wound. No indentations that would indicate teeth."

"But based on what we saw yesterday and what was on the video?"

Kevin nodded. "Could be. That thing's mouth looked almost beak-like to me. Without being able to get a closer look at the creature itself, my best educated guess is that they could be a match."

"A beak," Maria said. "Some kind of bird?"

"First, a bird that large? Not possible."

"Given what we've seen, we have to reevaluate our idea of what is or isn't possible. I'm sure the people who watch Simon's Syfy original movies would love the idea of a giant carnivorous penguin."

"Uh, true enough, I suppose. But second, let's say it is a bird that size. It wouldn't be able to stay underwater indefinitely. Even if we assume that whatever made it so large has also affected other aspects of its physiology, it's doubtful that we'd ever find a bird with gills. It has to come up and find someplace to stay. I would think that people would have noticed a fifty-foot booby."

"I really, really want to make a joke right now."

"Please don't. Booby jokes got old for me decades ago."

"Okay, then let's brainstorm what else it could be. I suppose what we saw could have belonged to a giant squid. And that one comes with the bonus of actually seeming plausible."

"That still would have been pretty large even for a giant squid." He stared off into space for several moments. "A couple problems with that. First, there was no sign of tentacles."

"To be sure, there wasn't much of a sign of anything, given how fast it happened."

"But the way a squid or even an octopus's beak is oriented, we would have seen something. Second, the water was too shallow. A giant squid would only be in the deep ocean, and it's highly unlikely that, even if it did get to the surface, it would be so close to shore."

"So maybe we've got to change our thinking to something that *would* be close to the shore," Maria said.

"But I don't see how something that big would be in water so shallow."

"It's not that shallow."

"Shallow enough."

A thought suddenly occurred to Maria. She probably would have had it earlier if she hadn't been recovering from her episode. "It's stationary."

"Seemed to move pretty fast to me."

"Sure, but it wasn't going very far from the island. And we saw it in just the same area where Debbie Schmidt disappeared."

"I don't know if that really gives us much help."

Maria snorted. "Maybe our problem is we're being too logical. We're trying to approach this from a scientific, real world perspective. Maybe we left that all behind one giant shark ago."

"Now you're the one sounding like Simon."

"Ugh. I know." She looked back down at the arm. "Speaking of which, one of us should try to find them. It's kind of weird that they've both wandered off for this long. Are we done here?"

"I'd like to stay here and see if there's anything more I can find, but if you want to get going, you could always talk to Merchant about pulling those strings and then go to the CDRS. Somewhere along the line, you'll have to find the Gutsdorfs. Puerto Ayora may be a tourist trap, but in the end it's not that big of a village."

"Fine. Let's pack the samples in a cooler and I'll take them."

"Maybe try to see a few sights while you're out. This whole trip is supposed to be at least sort of relaxing for you, remember."

Maria snorted. "Kevin, I think we lost all possibility of that last night."

12

Despite her words, Maria looked forward to having some of the day to herself and enjoying the fact that she was here, even if the islands were slowly on their way away from the heart of scientific inquiry that she had expected and toward being a tourist trap. If nothing else, she could be a tourist, at least for a little while.

They were right that Merchant could pull some strings with the Charles Darwin Research Station, but one thing she couldn't get from them was permission to film on their premises. Had the cast and crew of Sea Avenger come only six months earlier, the faculty at the CDRS probably would have been happy participate in anything that got their mission of preservation in front of the public. But the last people who had filmed there, apparently, had claimed they were part of a nature documentary, only for every scientist there to be surprised when the movie came out in limited release, heavily edited to make it seem like they all refuted the idea that evolution was true. As a result, the administrators at the CDRS were justifiably squirrely about the prospect of being on camera without more time for the filmmaker to be vetted. Maria would have thought Kevin's name and clout were enough, but still she understood their wish to be careful. She knew full well the power of something filmed then manipulated by and for a public more interested in twenty-second clips on YouTube than an honest scientific process. Otherwise, she wouldn't be the freaking Sea Avenger.

The people at the research station did give her a brief tour as a courtesy to a fellow scientist, though, for which she was grateful. She was surprised at how little they had to work with. This was the preeminent scientific organization on one of the most famous scientific sites in the world. And yet it was obvious that they were understaffed and underfunded. At one point, one of the workers showed her the cabinet-sized incubators used for tortoise eggs. The worker explained that the gender of the tortoises when they hatched was determined by the temperature- if they were kept at or slightly below eighty-four degrees, the hatchlings would be male. Anything over and they would be female. When Maria asked to see the system they used to accomplish the all-important task of ensuring there were equal numbers of males and females, the worker gave her a rueful smile and showed her a jury-rigged blow dryer on the cabinet's top shelf.

The fact that she didn't have any cameras following her, at the moment, brought up her mood as she exited the main building. Pretty much everything she had seen so far only served to further enhance her initial impression that she was standing in a world in a state of flux, not quite wilderness but far from metropolitan, part salt-of-the-earth folks trying to make their lives at the end of the world and part big business slowly seeping in to commodify it all and make a buck. On her way here, on a veranda outside a tiny hole-in-the-wall bar, a band of gray-haired older men had merrily playing away in a musical style Maria couldn't identify. Across the street from it was a very new looking building advertising day cruises from one of the largest entertainment corporations in the world. She'd seen the cruise ship out in the harbor, where it dwarfed all the dilapidated but well-loved fishing boats. Now here she was, standing among tourists in a landscape that was only a few steps above desert as they waited for a bus to take them further up into the Isla Santa Cruz Highlands to see the namesakes of the islands, the giant tortoises.

Come on, Maria, this has always been one of your dreams, she thought to herself. *Now that you're here, what are you going to do with it?*

Well, she sure as hell didn't want to do any of the really touristy stuff like parasailing, that was for sure. This was the Galápagos, damn it. She wanted to see animals. She wanted that same inspiration that Darwin had felt when he'd come upon birds and lizards so unused to humans that they would let him come up to them and push them aside with little more an annoyed squawk. Darwin had even told a story in *The Voyage of the Beagle* of how he had thrown a marine iguana out to sea, only for it to swim directly back to him several times, since it had seen the water as far more dangerous than the peculiar primate creature that kept picking it up and throwing it for no apparent reason. She'd seen a few animals, of course. She'd even seen some of the islands' better-known denizens. But the tortoises, the most iconic creatures on the whole of the islands, she hadn't witnessed yet.

She had to see some, she decided, even if she had to pretend to be a clichéd tourist to do it.

She found the first tour group that advertised it would be going into the highlands and joined up. While she was waiting for the small bus that would take them to arrive, she heard someone calling her name from outside the tour office. When she poked her head outside, she saw Simon and Cindy Gutsdorf walking down the middle of the road. Even though this was one of the most important and traveled sites on the islands, the road was still dirt, and there wasn't exactly a lot of traffic for them to avoid.

"Where the hell have you two been?" Maria asked. "Merchant has been getting salty without her jester to give her filler footage."

"Don't encourage him, please," Cindy said. "He's insufferable enough as it is without him getting it in his head that he's the star of the thing."

"Nah, I know how it works. The comic relief is never the hero." He released a massive sigh that, despite her best attempt, Maria couldn't decide if it was serious or intentionally ridiculous.

"Really, though, where were you?" Maria asked.

Cindy held up her hands to indicate the fresh open air of the island. "If we're going to be here for a while, then we wanted to enjoy it. What about you?"

"Same. Want to join me? I was about to take one of the tours to the turtle sanctuary."

"Why would you want to do that?" Simon asked. "You're a TV star. Ish. You could probably get in without all the people."

"Maybe I don't want to play that particular card any-more than I have to."

Maria was grateful when the small bus arrived and they all clamored on. She'd been on her feet, or rather foot, all morning and she was ready for a break. Not long ago, this much exertion wouldn't have tired her out at all. She found that walking around now, though, often used different muscles than she was used to, not to mention that, whether it was custom fitted for her or not, her prosthetic had a tendency to chafe something fierce when her stump was sweaty. The bus took them over a dirt road to an area back beyond the CDRS.

"Weren't you just already talking to the people at the research station?" Cindy asked. "Even without acting the celebrity, couldn't you have still just asked them to see the tortoises they have there? You wouldn't have needed to go into the highlands for that."

"Uh, they were friendly, but they didn't seem to want me around for too long. They didn't seem too keen on the idea that cameras might show up at any minute. And besides, I don't want to see giant tortoises in enclosures. I want to see the ones that have been reintroduced to their rightful place on the island. I want to see them in their natural habitat. Wait. How did you know that I'd already talked to the people in the station?"

There was a pause before Cindy answered. It was barely noticeable, but Maria was sure it was there. "We ran into Kevin as we were going through the village. He told us the general direction to find you and what you were doing."

"Huh," Maria said. Something about this exchange bothered her, but she didn't let it occupy too much space in her head. Instead, she took a strange glee in the way the bus bounced over the rougher patches of road. It almost felt like she was a kid again, on a field trip to some out of the way place to see something brand new and amazing for the first time.

The ride into the highlands took about half an hour, but to Maria, it was half an hour well spent. She'd thought Isla Niña was the Galápagos of her imagination, but that was a fairly barren rock. This was Isla Santa Cruz, the second largest island in the archipelago, and the farther they drove from Puerto Ayora, the more the land outside the windows transformed into something like the lost world of Darwin she'd always pictured. Although El Chato Tortoise Reserve, their destination, was an open area that tourists were allowed to move around freely, there was a man at the front talking in a heavy Ecuadorian accent and giving basic facts about the tortoises. Most of these Maria already knew, but every time he said something she didn't, she felt giddy, like each random factoid was the ultimate pearl of wisdom. Although she had expected to wander off by herself, she decided to stick close by their tour guide and see what else she could pick up.

Hell, maybe this tourist thing wasn't so bad after all.

The bus stopped in a patch of verdant semi-jungle and thick mist, which only added to Maria's growing excitement as they all filed off the bus.

"It's too bad none of the cameras are here," Cindy said to her. "Merchant would probably kill for footage of you acting like this. You're practically bouncing."

"Oh hush," Maria said. "Yeah, sure, sometimes you forget that the cameras are even there, but this is my time. I get to have a moment of joy that I don't have to share with the rest of the world."

"Please, follow me, there is much to show," their tour guide said. He looked to be in his early twenties, very slim, and for some reason dressed more for what Maria would have considered an office setting than a walking tour of the Galápagos wilds. He did, however, at least have a nametag that simply identified him as Al from All Greatness Tours.

Maria frowned. She hadn't paid much attention to which of the tour companies she'd gone with. She'd figured one was the same as any other. That name, though, seemed a little out of place.

Al led them down a few muddy inclines. Maria had trouble with some of them, but none of them were as difficult as her frustrating attempts to climb onto Isla Niña. In fact, Simon stumbled several times where Maria herself was able to keep her balance. It gave her a weird sense of satisfaction, the knowledge that, at least in some situation, she was getting so used to using one real leg and one fake that she could walk better than her companions with two legs each. It would just take time. She would get the hang of this.

Al chattered amiably as he led them past a lava tube, a large hole extending at a slight angle into the ground. The opening was so overgrown with vegetation that Maria almost didn't see it, but once she looked past the plants, she could see that it ran deep. As Al explained, and Maria already knew, these tubes could be found all over the islands, having been formed by the same volcanoes that brought the Galápagos into existence. There were probably quite a few, in remote places, that no one had even discovered yet.

"Some say these tubes are millions of years old," Al said. Something about the way he said it made clear that he wasn't a fan of the idea. Before anyone could ask him to talk about it further, though, he was again leading them away.

Then they reached a large, flat expanse of land. And there, slowly hobbling through the mists, were giants.

Maria stopped in her tracks, her breath caught in her throat. The first tortoise she saw lumbered in her general direction for a moment before it stopped and snaked its head out to rip off a number of leaves from a nearby bush. She'd known intellectually that the tortoises were enormous, but that knowing was different than seeing it for herself. From the bottom of its feet to the top of its shell the tortoise was taller than her hips. Its long slender neck was comparable to her forearm. Her mind wanted to reject the idea that such a large, unwieldy creature could move, yet move it did, its stubby legs patiently finding their footing as it walked closer in search of more food.

"It's magnificent," Maria whispered.

"Eh. I've seen bigger," Simon said.

"Oh yeah? Where?" Cindy asked.

"Um, it was on a television show."

"Fictional?"

"Yes. So? What does it matter? I've still seen bigger."

"You two really have a knack for ruining any moment, you know that?" Maria asked. She didn't look at either of them, though. The tortoise had plodded its way to be only fifteen feet from them now, and still it didn't seem to notice or care about their presence. She remembered another story Darwin had told about what had happened when he got close enough to one of the tortoises. It had hissed and abruptly pulled itself all the way into its shell. Darwin had then climbed on its back, rapped on the back of the shell, and the tortoise had come back out to go about its business, carrying Darwin around as though the man weren't even there. Maria doubted that anything like that would ever be allowed, but the child in her could fantasize.

Their guide Al came up next to Maria along with the rest of the tour group. "Here is a saddleback tortoise, called because of the distinct saddle shape of its shell, instead of a dome like some others. There are multiple subspecies of giant tortoise on the islands. You will find many different types here in the highlands because of the breeding efforts of the research station, but when Charles Darwin first came to the islands, the local governor boasted that he tell which island a tortoise had come from just by the shape of its shell. There are many who have treated this as further proof of Darwin's ideas about evolution."

Something about the tortoise seemed eerily familiar. Maria was so busy trying to figure out what it was that she almost missed what the tour guide said next. "Of course, it is now a well-known fact that Darwin was wrong."

Wait, what?

Maria looked around at her fellow tourists. One or two nodded their heads, but most looked just as confused as her. "I'm sorry, what do you mean by that?" Maria asked.

"We know now that the complexity of life is too great to have happened through an evolutionary process. While Darwin did his best with the information he had, we now see all the many ways in which his thinking was flawed."

"Um, no we don't," Maria said.

"Ma'am, please. I am an expert. I know what I am talking about."

"And I'm an actual biologist, and just because there were a few holes in Darwin's methodology doesn't mean that others didn't come along and fill them in. Natural selection can be observed in a human's lifetime, and has been seen right here on the islands using the finches."

Al straightened up. "Ma'am, you are being disruptive and interfering with the enjoyment of the others. If you do not stop, I will have to ask you to go back to the bus and wait."

"But what you're saying is actual, provable nonsense."

"Ma'am, you must go back to the bus. If not, I will be forced to call the police when we get back to Puerto Ayora."

"Uh, and what law am I breaking? This is… is…" She trailed off as the tortoise's neck extended to reach a leaf high on a nearby bush.

"Ma'am?"

"I… I guess I'll go back to the bus," she said. All the fight was gone from her voice, and she sounded distant even to herself. She took a step back, trying to go back in the direction of the bus without taking her eyes off the tortoise. She stumbled, and Simon had to catch her, but she barely noticed.

She was too entranced by the tortoise's long, wrinkly neck, the way it seemed to unbunch as the creature extended its head, and the tough, beak-like mouth it used to rip off the leaves.

As much as she had wanted to come out here and see the tortoises, she was suddenly anxious to get back to Puerto Ayora and Kevin.

Because she thought she knew now what might be living in the waters of Isla Niña.

13

"A tortoise?" Merchant asked, her voice halfway between disbelief and giddy glee. Maria was sure she was having visions of ridiculously high ratings dancing through her head. "You think Mrs. Schmidt was eaten by a giant, mutant tortoise?"

They were all gathered in *Sea Avenger*'s bungalow command center. Immediately after the bus had dropped them off back in Puerto Ayora, Maria had run (it wasn't until later that she realized this was the first time she had run since she'd lost her leg, and she was surprised by the ease with which she'd accomplished it) back to the bungalow and ordered everyone to gather around. Ernesto was here, and Kevin had arrived with Monica and Gutierrez shortly before Maria and the Gutsdorfs. They were gathered in a loose circle, with all the camera people and sound engineers and general production hangers-on trying to make sure they captured every moment of this meeting without actually getting in the shot.

"Not a mutant," Maria said. "Well, actually yes. No. Maybe. We can't know yet. The DNA samples we got off the arm might be able to help us with its exact origin."

"A giant tortoise or turtle, though?" Kevin asked. "You don't think that sounds at all far-fetched?"

"No. Given the fact that we're in the Galápagos, an environment known for producing not only giant tortoises but also for forcing natural selection to work faster than other places, I'd say that's substantially less far-fetched than, say, an enormous hammerhead that can control other sharks."

"Fair enough point," Kevin said. "But this still requires us to jump to some conclusions without having many facts. I thought you wanted to be Scully instead of Mulder."

"Did I say I was Scully?" Maria asked. "I thought I was Mulder."

"You obviously aren't sure because the writer can't remember what she wrote earlier," Simon said.

Maria, Kevin, and Cindy all turned to him and spoke at once. "Shut up, Simon."

Simon hmphed.

"Look, we can review the tapes again, but we've all already seen them plenty of times. Whatever was under the water was long and kind of snaked out. That was its neck. And what little we could see of its mouth matches that of a turtle or tortoise."

"I see several problems with that assertion," Ernesto said. "The first is that the tortoises of the Galápagos are vegetarians. There is no way one would eat a tourist, even if it did somehow grow to that size."

"There are meat eaters in the turtle and tortoise family, though," Maria said. "We can't make the assumption that this one is a native to the area. It might not be a direct descendant of any Galápagos species of tortoise or sea turtle. It could have been introduced."

"And how exactly would someone 'introduce' something big enough to eat a person whole without anyone seeing?" Cindy asked.

"I don't know," Maria asked. "Maybe that's something we can look into. You know, like seeing if anyone has noticed anyone or anything suspicious about Isla Niña before this."

"I could look into that," Ernesto said.

"There's also the issue of where something of that size is hiding," Kevin said. "If it's a turtle or tortoise, then it has to breathe air. It couldn't just stay below the water at all times where it couldn't be seen."

"Maybe whatever made it so much bigger also changed its lung capacity," Maria said.

"I suppose that's believable," Kevin said. "There are any number of species that have evolved tricks that keep them from needing to breathe air for long times and let them go to great depths. Still, it has to come up eventually, and anything that big coming up to the surface should have been noticed before now."

Maria shrugged. "I can't guess yet where it might be hiding, but I've got a hypothesis as to why it's only now presenting itself."

"And that is?" Kevin asked.

"It ran out of food."

Kevin thought about that for several seconds. "Yes. Yes, that would make sense."

"Not to me, it doesn't," Merchant said. "Care to explain your thinking to the cameras?"

"The missing sea lions," Kevin said. "Wherever it came from, however long it's been here, up until now the sea lions must have been its primary source of nourishment. That's why we didn't find the large harems we should have on Isla Niña. It ate them."

"We need to come up with something better to call it than 'it,'" Simon said. "It needs a name."

"No," Cindy said. "No way. The last time you came up with a name for a giant monster of the deep, you named it Teddy Bear."

"I say, Call It George," Simon said, ignoring his sister.

"George as in named after the tortoise Lonesome George?" Maria asked. The tortoise in question had been the last of his sub-species and had died several years ago. His only legacy on the island now was as an image used to sell souvenirs.

"No, not George. Call It George. As in 'I will hug it and pet it and squeeze it and call it George.' That way we can have a 'Who's on first' moment every time someone uses its name."

"We are not calling it Call It George," Maria said.

"Aw shit," Cindy said, putting her head in her hands.

"What?" Maria asked.

"By flat out stating that we're not calling it Call It George, you've pretty much just guaranteed that's what we're going to call it."

Everyone else in the circle nodded, even some of the production crew. That was, after all, pretty much the unspoken rule.

"Fine. Whatever. We're stuck with Call It George," Maria said. "Can we get back on track, please?"

Monica snorted. "You mean we were ever on track to begin with?"

"Sea lions," Maria said. "That was what was providing George with—"

"Call It George," Simon corrected.

"Oh for fuck's sake. That was what was providing Call It George with its food. But it's too big for such a small island and food source. It ate all of them, so it had to adapt. It had to start eating other things. Like the iguana we saw."

"And, when the opportunity presented itself, tourists," Kevin said.

"So that's it?" Merchant asked. "That's the mystery solved?"

"No, that's a hypothesis presented," Kevin said. "Before we can get anyone to agree to permanently closing Isla Niña down to tourist traffic again, we need proof beyond blurry video footage."

"Why not just kill the son of a bitch?" Gutierrez asked.

"Same reason we tried to avoid killing Teddy Bear," Kevin said. "Whatever this is, it's likely a brand new species or sub-species, and we're biologists. We're not in the business of exterminating endangered creatures."

"Yes, because that policy worked out so well last time," Gutierrez said, indicating Maria's leg. "No offense."

"Only a little taken," Maria said. "Look, I understand anyone's wish to kill something that scary, okay? If I were face to face with Teddy Bear again, I can't say that I wouldn't try to take her out. But we need to be scientists here, okay? And a scientist doesn't go up to the only known member of a species and kill it unless they have to."

"So what's the plan instead?" Cindy asked.

"We need to go back to Isla Niña and get better proof. More video footage would be good, but the best would be a definite DNA sample. Anything at all that can tell us what exactly Call It George is, and how it got here. This is huge, everyone. This could be bigger than Teddy Bear."

"Um, are you meaning that figuratively or literally?" Simon asked.

"Yes," Kevin said with a smile.

"Mayor Estevez probably won't be very happy about anything that would keep Isla Niña of the tourists' itineraries," Ernesto said.

"Yeah, well, I don't give two tiny constipated shits what that man wants," Maria said.

"Gutierrez, why don't you head back to the *Cameron*, and make sure she's refueled and ready to go," Kevin said. "We'll leave in about two hours."

"Are you sure it's wise to be out there with Call It George once it gets dark?" Monica asked.

"So far, we don't have any evidence that it strays too far from Isla Niña, for whatever reason. We'll anchor the *Cameron* with just enough distance that we'll be safe, yet close enough to try observing it. We won't make any more serious attempt to study it until the morning."

"I'm on it, boss," Gutierrez said.

Maria looked at the Gutsdorfs. "You two want to follow him and make sure all the equipment is stowed properly?"

The circle began to break up, and the TV crew took that as their cue to prepare their own equipment for the next trip out to the island. Ernesto looked like he was about to head out as well, but Maria caught him by the arm before he got to the door.

"Hey, I actually wanted to ask you something," Maria said.

"Go right ahead."

"Uh, so when I went out to the highlands to see the tortoises this funny thing happened…"

She didn't even have to finish before Ernesto put his forehead in his hands and shook his head. "Which tour group did you use? Was it Galápagos Alive?"

"Uh, no. The company was called All Greatness."

"That would have been my second guess. I wish you would have asked me for a recommendation. I could have given you the names of plenty of tour guides who weren't going to try telling you your life's work was the work of El Diablo, or whatever the hell Al was preaching today."

"So, that's common?"

"Miss Quintero, it's more than common. There are many people in the Galápagos that believe Darwin was, at best, misguided, or at worst, an agent of Satan."

Monica wandered over to join them, listening with a frown on her face.

"But this is the Galápagos Freaking Islands, for Christ's sake," Maria said. "The biggest and best proof in the world that evolution and natural selection are true. How can there be people here who just ignore that?"

"What are you trying to say, that just because people believe in God they must be ignorant?" Monica asked. "Because I've got to warn you, I'm a Catholic and I would take offense to that."

"Really?" Maria asked. "I guess you've never mentioned it before."

"Does it surprise you?" Monica asked.

"A little bit."

"Well, don't be. I can be religious and scientific at the same time. I believe and God and Jesus, yet still acknowledge evolution as true."

"I myself am a Methodist," Ernesto said. "And I agree with you."

"Okay, point taken," Maria said. "I didn't mean it to sound like I was anti-religion. But…"

"But groups like All Greatness and Galápagos Alive are spreading provably false information," Ernesto said.

"Exactly," Maria said. "How does that even happen?"

"All I can say is welcome to the Galápagos," Ernesto said. "There are a huge influx of outside forces now, and little to no regulation over any of it. The same lack of competent leadership that led to overfishing in protected waters and unrestrained tourist trade resulted in certain groups seeing opportunities. Galápagos Alive is actually funded by an American mega-church. You're lucky you didn't use them instead. They probably would have blatantly branded you as an apostate or something right in front of the whole tour group. All Greatness at least is a purely family run business, second generation Galapaguenos, but also heavily influenced by certain missionaries."

"But this is the Galápagos. Surely these people can't deny evolution when faced with evidence of it every day."

"Remember that influx of money I told you about? Guess how much of it goes to local education. There are a significant number of the native population who only know Darwin as that man with his name on everything. Whatever Al might have said on the tour about Darwin? There was nothing deliberately misleading about it. Al and others like him have been told that evolution is a lie meant to lead humanity astray, or something like that, and no one has ever shown them how to connect the dots in their environment to see the real picture."

"So wait, all of this money coming into the Galápagos from the tourist trade, and none of it goes into education?"

"No. Most of it just goes into the pockets of companies whose CEOs will never even set foot on the islands. Some goes into the pockets of certain politicians. Only a small portion of the millions of dollars flowing through the archipelago actually go to the people who have to live here."

"Isn't there anything we can do about it?" Maria asked.

Ernesto gave a humorless laugh. "We? Are you now a Galápagos native?"

"No, but I'm someone who cares about the islands."

"And also someone who will be gone in less than a week. No offense, Miss Quintero. I like you. I have not seen anything so far that doesn't lead me to respect you. But just because your skin is not white doesn't mean you're not acting like hundreds of white wannabe saviors who have come to the Galápagos before. We, and by 'we' I mean the residents of the islands, will solve our own problems. Thank you for the offer, but just because we're on islands in the middle of nowhere doesn't mean we aren't our own people."

"Right. You're right. Sorry."

"Apology accepted. I assure you, I'm not alone in wanting change. There are others who want what's best for the people of the islands without losing what makes the Galápagos unique. Now if you'll excuse me, I have a few people I can hit up for information on anything suspicious at Isla Niña."

14

The *Cameron* anchored for the night within sight of Isla Niña, and although they were all reasonably certain that they were far enough away that Call It George wouldn't disturb them, someone stayed on watch duty all through the night. Even the camera people joined in on the rotation, each of them equipped with night vision video equipment in the hope they would catch more evidence of the Isla Niña monster. They didn't, but there were multiple reports from other watchers of large disturbances in the water right about where they had last seen the creature. It was definitely out there, and for whatever reason, it would only stay in one place.

For Maria, the night was longer than any other since the Cortez Incident. She couldn't sleep, even though Kevin did his cute little snore next to her. Mostly because her leg hurt, the one that no longer existed. Every time she heard a particularly large splash against the side of the *Cameron*, her entire body tensed up against her will, as though it thought something was going to come crashing through the walls for her.

I can't keep going on like this, Maria thought, but she had no idea how to deal with it. She finally found something that only partially resembled a fitful sleep when she pulled out a small flashlight and propped it in such a way that it shone directly on her bare left foot. Somehow, that sight was comforting.

In the morning, the *Cameron* bustled with pent-up energy. There was a general feel among everyone, unspoken but very evident among both the normal crew and the TV people, that this was the day they had been building towards. Maria tried to revel in the energy like everyone else, but all she could feel was a dull buzz in the back of her head, like an alarm clock that had been shoved under a pillow but still wouldn't stop.

Kevin joined her as she stood on the deck, white-knuckling the railing as she stared out at the spot of ocean where they'd seen

Call It George. "You doing okay?" he asked.

"I'm fine."

"Now let's try the truth."

"The boat's not even moving and I think I'm going to puke. Some action heroine I am."

"I figured as much. I'm actually here on behalf of Merchant. She figured it might be easier for you if I was the one who passed along her message."

"Is this a message I'm going to want to hear?"

"No."

"Are you going to do it anyway?"

"Yes."

"Give it to me straight then."

"She says she wants you to take point on anything we do today."

"And what exactly will we be doing today?"

"Basically, we're going to try luring Call It George out for a clear camera shot. We've got some meat we'll be throwing in the water. We'll keep our distance as much as possible, but it will still require someone to get fairly close in one of the Zodiacs."

"So I'm basically expected to go face to face with this thing?"

"That's what Merchant wants, yeah. She said she needs a shot of you being heroic if she's going to give this whole thing the narrative spin she needs."

Maria snorted. "What, she can't do anything with the shots Gary and Charlene got of me freaking out?"

"I'm assuming that's a rhetorical question you don't need me to answer."

"Yes, it is. So what happens if I can't? What happens if I can't get in that Zodiac and get the shot of me feeding a sea monster?"

Kevin didn't answer right away.

"Kevin?" she asked.

He sighed. "She claims it's not her decision, but the network's. She's been in contact with them this whole time, of course. They know about Call It George, and they know about what happened. And if they don't get the heroic Maria Quintero they believe they signed a contract for…" He trailed off.

"Yes?"

"Then it's no longer your show. It's back to the original plan of the show centering around me."

Maria let out a deep breath. "That's not so bad."

"That was what I thought, too, but it means you would no longer be the one making the big money. Suddenly, all those medical bills are back on the plate."

"If I asked for your help with them, though, you would, right?"

"Of course I would. But I also know you. You wouldn't ask."

"No, I probably wouldn't."

They stood in silence for several moments as Maria considered this. Out across the crystal blue waters of the Galápagos, the sea around Isla Niña was calm. There was no sign at the moment that anything uncanny might be hiding below the waves.

"It's the tide," Kevin said as though he could read her thoughts. Apparently, they'd been a couple long enough where they could do that freaky I-know-what-my-partner-is-really-thinking trick. "We made a chart this morning while you were still in bed. Every appearance we've had so far, even just the hard-to-see extra splashing during the night, has been during low tide. I think that might be a way to make this whole thing safer. We go in and throw out the bait before it gets to low tide, and we wait nearby with the cameras."

"Sounds like a good plan," she said then, after taking a deep breath, added what she had already known she would say throughout the whole conversation. "Too bad it's a plan I can't be a part of."

"I had a feeling all along that you were going to say that. Are you sure, though?"

"Nope. Not sure at all. That's the problem. You saw the way I was the other night. For several seconds there, I was absolutely convinced that Teddy Bear was coming for me. Nothing would convince me otherwise. It's dangerous, and I can't force it on anyone else. That wouldn't be the right thing to do."

"There are still other ways we can do this. Hell, I bet with some camera trickery, we can even make it look like you're closer than you really are. We'll just need to use both Zodiacs…"

"No. No trickery. Reality or nothing at all. It's time we both face the facts: I wasn't ready for this. I pushed too hard, and I came out here when I wasn't mentally prepared. If I keep pushing, then who knows? Someone could get killed. And I can't have that."

Kevin nodded. "Do you know why I love you?"

"Because I know the best way to use a riding crop?"

"Besides that. I love you because I knew you would say that." He gently kissed her on the temple. "I'll go tell Merchant. No one will fault you if you go back down below deck."

"No. I can watch you play the hero, at least. Give me that much credit."

She stood off to the side as the others inflated one of the Zodiacs, then loaded it with supplies. They didn't need much: a cooler full of meat that was just as likely to attract the local white-tipped reef sharks as it was their quarry, equipment to steady a camera, a long pole with a needle on the end that they hoped to use to collect a DNA sample. Although no one expected to need it, Kevin also included a scuba tank on the off chance that he thought he needed to dive to attract Call It George. Personally, Maria thought that last bit was pointless. If he ended up in the water with something capable of swallowing someone whole, it was too late for him to do anything except possibly bleed to death.

While Kevin put on his wetsuit, there was some discussion among the TV people about who would be in the Zodiac with Kevin and who would film from the *Cameron*. Merchant eventually decided that she wanted her more experienced camera people trying to get the wide shot from as many angles as possible, which left Ted Shirr to go in the Zodiac. As soon as this was announced, Maria heard Simon snickering quietly to himself off to the side.

"What's funny?"

"Oh, nothing."

"No, really. What?"

"It's just the writer of our show is displaying her sense of humor again."

"I don't get it."

"Never mind," Simon said, then walked away before she could further press him for an explanation.

"Okay, looks like everything is ready," Simon said once Ted was in his own wetsuit. "Time to get moving if we want to do this when the tide is right."

Before he got on the Zodiac, Maria gave him a kiss. "Go get the money shot."

"I'm not sure if that phrase means what you think it means."

"I know what it means. And if you get this shot, I'll make sure you see the other kind later."

He smiled. "Looking forward to it."

As the Zodiac motored away from the *Cameron*, Simon and Cindy came up to her. "That wasn't actually very smart," Simon said.

"What wasn't?"

"Getting cutesy with him immediately before he goes into danger."

"Jesus, Simon, shut it," Cindy said, but Maria couldn't help but notice a sudden worried tone in her voice.

"Simon, that doesn't mean anything's going to happen," Maria said. "What would it take to convince that we are not in some kind of work of fiction?"

"Well, for starters, nothing bad could happen right now," Simon said. "In fact, Call It George would have to not even show up. Because there's nothing story worthy about that."

Monica, who had been watching the Zodiac from nearby with a pair of binoculars, called out. "Hey, I think I see something moving in the water."

Maria turned to Simon. "Sometimes I think I kind of hate you a little."

"Shit," Cindy said. She tapped her fingernails on the railing for a moment in thought, then turned to the stairs, grabbing her brother's shirtsleeve and tugging him along with her. "Come on, little boy."

"Where are we going?" Simon asked.

"Lord help me, I'm taking you seriously for once." They were gone before Maria could ask her to clarify what she meant.

The Zodiac had begun to approach the spot where they'd seen the mouth come up out of the water, but it stopped short at what Kevin must have thought was a safe distance. He apparently saw Monica frantically gesturing at him and looked to the dark shadow that had appeared in the water closer to the island. In the daylight, it was easier to see that, whatever Call It George might be, it was massive, bigger than they had initially thought.

"Which might mean it's longer, too," Maria whispered with a deep sense of dread growing in her stomach.

Ted pointed his camera at the shape in the water while Kevin slowly yet pointedly maneuvered the Zodiac away. From this distance, it was difficult to tell what the shadow might be doing, but Kevin's posture slackened. He didn't seem to think there was any danger.

Shit, Maria thought. She knew exactly what came next.

To the best of her knowledge, the mysterious shadow beneath the crystal blue waters never moved. Maybe they were wrong. Maybe that hadn't been Call It George after all. It couldn't be, really, because Call It George came at the Zodiac from a completely different direction. Kevin didn't even have the time to turn as the water beneath and behind him suddenly boiled with violence.

It's happening again, Maria thought. *She's back. She's here. It's Teddy Bear with the same tricks.* Her scarred mind continued to insist that even as the thing rose up out of the water. It was fast, yet not as fast as it had been the other night. All of the cameras, except probably for poor Ted's, caught an image of it crystal clear.

She'd been right. Call It George obviously had some relationship to a turtle or tortoise, although it was also evident that it didn't quite belong to either family. Its mouth wasn't quite as large as Maria remembered from the other night, but it was still large enough that it could lift the Zodiac up in its wickedly sharp grayish-green beak. The skin beyond the beak was mottled and scaled, and the thing had two jet-black eyes each the size of a human head.

The thing almost looked familiar, and it took Maria a second to realize why: that old Japanese monster movie. What had it been called? Oh, right. Gamera.

Her boyfriend was about to be eaten by a baby Gamera.

Its jaws were open wide enough that it could almost but not quite grip the Zodiac from both sides as it lifted the raft into the air. For a moment, the gigantic head and long neck hung there, almost in defiance of gravity. Ted appeared to be screaming even as he tried to point the camera at what was below them. Kevin also looked panicked, but unlike Ted, he didn't act it. Maria saw him reach for the scuba tank and desperately try to get the rebreather into his mouth.

Then Call It George's mouth snapped shut.

In her head, Maria imagined an audible crunching noise, but it never came. The material of the Zodiac folded over on Kevin and Ted, wrapping them up yet preventing Call It George from getting a decent grip on them. That didn't appear to matter to it, though, as the moment it looked to have any kind of hold at all on the boat the creature yanked its head back down below the water, pulling its two neatly wrapped victims down with it.

The *Cameron* erupted with a chorus of screaming. *I wonder how many more times we have to see that kind of thing before people on this boat stop doing that*, Maria idly thought, right before realizing that her own voice was among the plaintive cries.

"Kevin!" she screamed. "Oh my God, Kevin!"

The water stopped churning. For several seconds, they could still see several dark silhouettes below the water, and then they faded into the blue.

"Gutierrez!" Maria yelled, not even sure exactly where he was. "Get the *Cameron* closer! We have to get them!"

From somewhere else on the deck, she heard him say, "But that thing could..."

"Now, you asshole!"

For many precious seconds, nothing happened. She had a vague awareness that Monica and the TV people were frantic and screaming, and some of them might have even been asking her what they should do, but Maria couldn't move. She simply kept her gaze on the place where the Zodiac had disappeared, waiting, hoping, knowing something would likely come up and wishing that whatever it was, it wasn't just a body part. When the *Cameron* finally moved, her paralysis broke. She ran to the side of the boat where it would pull up along where they had disappeared. Seconds before they got there, she thought she saw shape rising to the surface from below.

"Oh God, it's coming back!" Gary yelled.

"No, it's too small," Maria said. Too small to be a giant mutant turtle, but just the right size to be…

"Kevin?" she whispered.

The wet-suit clad body hit the surface, face down. Maria didn't see any blood, and the body seemed to be whole, but there was no movement. Whichever one of them it was, he appeared to be dead.

"Monica, get the first-aid kit!" Maria said. "Charlene, put down the fucking camera and grab one of those poles over there with the hoops on them."

Merchant's voice was a whisper near her ear. "Maria, I don't think…"

"Everyone just get your asses moving! We can still save him."

Maria helped Charlene with the pole, and together they were able to wrangle the body onto the deck. Their combined strength gave out as they pulled him over the railing, and he flopped limply onto his back on the deck. She'd been right. He wasn't breathing.

He also wasn't Kevin.

Ted's lips and skin were blue, but he probably hadn't been in the water so long that he was beyond saving. Maria mentally psyched herself up to give him CPR, but Monica was on her knees next to him before she could get there.

"Shit," Maria heard from behind her. She turned to see that Cindy and Simon had returned to the deck, a plastic tote held between the two of them. She didn't take any time to check and see what they had thought was so important.

"Everyone give Monica some room," Maria said.

"You shouldn't bother," Simon said.

"Simon! Jesus! Learn when to shut up," Cindy responded.

"Look, it's a tragedy, but it was obvious he was going to die from the beginning. I mean, his name was…"

Monica pulled away from Ted as he sputtered sea water and took a couple of deep, desperate breaths.

"Oh," Simon said, sounding almost disappointed. "I get it. The television writers are just messing with us again."

Maria didn't look at him, but she clearly heard Cindy smack him upside the head. She wanted to ask Ted what had happened, where Kevin was, but he was spending all his energy at the moment just remembering how his lungs worked. She ran over to the railing again, expecting that Kevin had bobbed up while they'd been distracted by Ted, but the water was empty.

Cindy came up next to her put a hand on her shoulder. "Maria, he…"

"Don't. Don't you dare say it. Don't you dare. He's not dead."

"That's not what she was going to say," Simon said as he came up on her other side. "She was going to say that he needs you to save him."

"Wait, what?"

She finally turned around and looked at the tote they had brought up from below. In it was a wetsuit, a scuba tank and rebreather, a single flipper, and a black plastic case that Maria recognized but hadn't brought herself to open yet. Cindy also carried a duffel bag with a few other things in it, while Simon had a harpoon gun.

"The whole story has been building up to this point, don't you see?" Simon asked.

"Jesus Christ, just stop it, Simon!" Maria said. "For the last God-damned time, we're not in fiction."

"How sure are you of that really?" Cindy asked.

Maria gave her a stunned look. "Please don't tell me you're buying into this."

"I don't think I am. But what if he's right?"

"He's not."

"But what if he is? That would make you the hero, and Kevin the love of your life, and this would be the point in the story where you have to overcome all your fears and obstacles to save him."

Maria looked from one to the other and then back again, her

mouth agape. The whole "maybe we're just in a TV show or movie" bit had been vaguely entertaining at one point, but now they were going overboard. She was real. They were all real. She refused to play the what-if game about this.

But there was one what-if she couldn't discount: what if Kevin really was alive? Ted hadn't been eaten, but he'd almost drowned. The last view of Kevin she'd had suggested that he might have gotten his rebreather in his mouth in time, and the folded-over Zodiac could have prevented the worst of the monster's bites from doing too much damage. Was it really too much to hope that Call It George had simply dragged him some place, that Kevin was alive but trapped and only needed her to overcome her personal demons?

Yes, it was too much to hope that.

But screw it. She was going to hope anyway.

"Alright," Maria said. "Help me suit up."

15

One thing that they could all agree on was that she didn't have a lot of time. The most logical conclusion was that Kevin was already dead, swallowed whole by Call It George and currently digesting in the creature's stomach. Not exactly an image Maria liked to think about, but there it was. On the very off chance that he was alive, though, they had to assume that he wouldn't be for much longer. If Call It George hadn't eaten him already, then it was probably saving him for something, and there was no way that something would be good or even in the distant future. Even if for some reason Call It George did not eat him for a while, there was still the matter of air. Kevin looked like he'd had the foresight to try the rebreather, but it could have been ripped away from him as he was dragged under, or the tank could have been damaged and had less air than it should have. No matter which way Maria looked at it, she had to move if there was to be even the slightest chance to get him out of this alive.

That meant she didn't have time for privacy as she stripped off her clothes and put on the wetsuit. Thankfully, for exactly this reason she had long ago taken to wearing a bikini under her clothes instead of underwear whenever she was on the *Cameron*, so at least she didn't flash the cameras as they caught the whole thing. Before she could put on the wet-suit, however, there was the matter of her prosthetic. She removed the one she'd been wearing, which had been designed for everyday walking and the occasional tough hike, and set it aside as Cindy pulled out the black plastic case they'd brought with them.

"How did you know to grab this?" Maria asked her.

"Merchant was talking about it the other day. She was saying she was afraid she'd never get this moment on film."

"Have you had a chance to test it out yet?" Simon asked.

"Nope. I haven't actually been back in the water since Cortez. Not even a swimming pool."

"This isn't exactly the best time to try it for the first time, is it?" Cindy asked.

"No, but think of it this way: me using it untested will look good for the cameras, both Merchant's real ones and Simon's imaginary ones."

Cindy undid the latches on the case and opened it. Merchant, although she was obviously very unnerved by all that was going on and looked like she'd rather drop everything to make sure that Ted was okay, continued to direct the camera crew, making sure they got a dramatic first shot of the case's contents.

It contained a leg.

Not a real one, of course. It was a prosthetic just like the one Maria had been wearing, but where that one was rather standard, this one was special. It had been 3-D printed using exact specifications provided by her and Kevin. It looked sleek next to her other one, a fancy sports car compared to a utilitarian truck. It was black plastic and carbon fiber, molded to fit her stump, and hinged in ways her other prosthetic wasn't. And instead of a foot at the end, it had an attached flipper that matched the other the Gutsdorfs had brought up.

This was Maria's own personal diving prosthetic, one of a kind.

Cindy pulled it out and tested the joints. "There better not be anything wrong with this."

"The company that made it for me offered a money back guarantee," Maria said.

"Well, you can't get your money back if you're eaten," Simon said.

Cindy smacked him. "Maybe talking about her getting eaten isn't the best for her mental state now?"

"Don't worry," Maria said, forcing a smile. "It's not my money anyway. The network bought it. If I die, they're the ones who benefit."

"Can I just state for the record that the network does not want you to die for any reason?" Merchant asked.

"What, no insurance on me?"

"Oh, you're insured out the yin-yang. But I'm sure that I speak for everyone from TEC when I say we don't actually want you do die. And it's not even a ratings thing."

"Thanks. I think." Maria strapped on the diving leg, detaching the fin long enough for her to get her wetsuit on over it, then put the fin back on. Cindy strapped the other fin to her other foot as Merchant came up to her.

"I want to strap a GoPro to your head, but your life isn't worth footage. If you think it will be too distracting at the worst time, just say so and we'll say screw the video."

"No, as long as it's not loose, I think that should be okay. I'll ditch it if I feel like I have to."

"Okay, look," Cindy said as she finished with the fin and went to the duffel she'd brought. "We've got a belt here with some flairs."

"The water's not deep enough here that I'll need them," Maria said.

"Maybe not, but I thought you could use them as a weapon if nothing else. Big or not, that thing probably wouldn't enjoy burning hot magnesium against its skin."

"Fair enough. What else do you have?"

Cindy pulled out a large knife in a sheath, along with a complicated strap. She put it around Maria's thigh as Maria hooked on the flairs. "If you have to go close quarters against that thing, you're probably screwed, but just in case."

"And then this," Simon said, holding out a harpoon gun. "So hopefully you don't have to get close at all."

Maria couldn't help but notice that no one was talking about not harming Call It George anymore. They all wanted to conserve this creature if they could, but when forced to choose between it and Kevin, there really wasn't any choice.

Cindy helped put the scuba tank on Maria's back as Monica led Ted over to them. He looked shell-shocked and was shivering like hell, but there didn't appear to be any permanent physical damage.

"Ted, did you see anything that could help me?" Maria asked. "Anything at all?"

"It tried to eat me," Ted whispered.

"I guess that's a no. Okay, everything ready?" she asked as she put on her goggles.

"As ready as it can be," Cindy said. "How about you?"

Maria grabbed onto the railing and prepared to flip over the side. "Yep. I'm…"

Maria froze.

Oh God, she thought. *Not now. I can't freeze up now.* She looked down at the water, seeing the quick blurs of shapes underneath the clear blue water, and while her logical brain told her there was nothing there but fish, her instinctual half told her that every single unknown shape was something enormous, something that had been waiting for her. Maybe Call It George, maybe Teddy Bear. She'd spilled her blood in the water before and now everything in the ocean with teeth wanted to finish her.

If I go into that water, I will never come back out, Maria thought.

"Maria?" Monica said. "Maria, you need to breath regularly."

I can't. I can't do this. Someone else has to go.

Except they had already wasted too much time. She was the only one suited up and ready to go.

If I go in, my rebreather won't work right. Water will fill my lungs. I'll sink. I'll die. Scavengers will nip the flesh off my corpse.

She wouldn't die. She'd done this hundreds of times. She was a pro. No one else on the *Cameron* had the same level of diving experience.

I can't, though. I won't. No one can make me.

No, no one could make her if she refused. But then, if he really was somehow alive, the man she loved would die for real.

There's a hole, she thought.

"She can't do it," Monica said. "Someone else needs to…"

"No," Maria said, surprised by the volume of her voice. "There's a hole."

"Huh?" Cindy asked.

"There's a hole, there's a hole, there's a hole at the bottom of the sea."

"Okay I think she's losing it," Simon said.

"There's a log, there's a log, there's a log in the hole at the bottom of the sea."

"No, wait, I think I know what she's doing," Monica said. "See? She's calming down."

"There's a branch, there's a branch, there's a branch on the log in the hole at the bottom of the sea."

With that, Maria put the rebreather in her mouth, made sure she had a tight grip on the harpoon gun, and then flipped over the railing into the water.

The temperature of the water was a shock to her system despite the wetsuit. She hadn't been in it for so long, after all, that she'd almost forgotten the sensation. It threatened to seep into her mind and make her panic, but she continued the mantra in her mind.

There's a twig, there's a twig, there's a twig on the branch on the log in the hole at the bottom of the sea.

As long as she kept up the mental litany, she thought she could control the impulses to panic. Right. So all she needed to do was hum a half-forgotten song from her childhood while she tried to save her boyfriend from a sea monster deep below the surface. Easy, right?

Actually, she realized, this wasn't that much harder than the last dive she'd done. Of course, the last dive had ended with her minus a leg, so maybe she should stop comparing them while she was ahead.

There's a frog, there's a frog, there's a frog on the twig on the branch on the log in the hole at the bottom of the sea.

At this point, she was pretty sure she had the song completely wrong, but it seemed to be doing the trick. She allowed herself to sink in the ocean and acclimate to being back in what she used to consider her home. She wasn't sure if it would ever truly be that home ever again, but she could try.

The world beneath her teemed with life, and it brought her further comfort that she could identify almost everything she saw. Anchovies, Moorish idols, yellow-tailed surgeonfish. Some distance off, she thought she could see a spotted eagle ray. The sea floor was a labyrinth of volcanic rocks covered in coral and algae. And everything around it was blue. So blue. A blue so deep it made the eyes hurt.

Oh right, she thought. *I do belong here.* She lost her place in the song, but she made no effort to find it. She thought she was okay again, at least for now.

She had no idea how long it took her to acclimate, but it felt too long. Tick-tock, after all. She dove deeper, still trying to get used to the bizarre sensation of being propelled by only one leg. The joints in the prosthetic were specially designed to mimic the motion of swimming and only that motion, so when she moved her stump, the prosthetic filled in the rest of the movements. Maria kept listing slightly to one side or the other, either forgetting or overcompensating for the prosthetic's help. As she dove lower and reached the bottom, though, she thought she had enough of a hang of it that she could function. Of course, if she got into a sticky situation, all bets were off.

And she was pretty positive that she would get into a sticky situation.

Maria hadn't entered the water with any other plan than *Save Kevin*. Now that she was here, she began to work the problem. Call It George lived here. It never appeared to venture from this part of the island. So logic dictated that it had to have a home here. Now, the ten million dollar question was, if she were an enormous mutant carnivorous sea turtle, where would she live?

In a hole at the bottom of the sea, she thought idly, then chided herself for being stupid.

She saw something resting in the algae and swam for a closer look. The item in front of her was so mangled that at first she couldn't identify it. Then her mind pieced it together and recognized it as Ted's camera. Looking up, she figured she was just a little landward from where the Zodiac had gone under, so this might just be the closest thing she would get to a breadcrumb trail. She continued in the direction of the island, stopping only once to freeze up as a white-tipped reef shark passed by.

There's a tail, there's a tail, there's a tail on the frog on the twig on the branch on the log in the hole at the bottom of the sea.

The shark was smaller than the ones that attacked her, and she wouldn't have registered to it as food, but nonetheless, she felt better when it was gone on its business. Assuming she got out of today's adventure in one piece (*unlike last time, ha-fricking-ha*), she was going to need to confront that phobia. It wouldn't do her any good to be a marine biologist that couldn't get near even the smallest shark.

As soon as she was close enough to see the base of the island itself underwater, it became obvious where she needed to go. While none had ever been discovered on the surface of the island, Maria now found herself facing an enormous underwater lava tube. The resulting cave disappeared back into the volcanic rock, and the sides looked like they had been worn smooth by something repeatedly passing in and out.

Well I'll be damned, Maria thought. *There really is a hole at the bottom of the sea. But if I find Call It George down there with a giant mutant frog, I'm calling shenanigans.*

If there was any doubt that this was the right place, Maria found the DNA collection prod just outside the entrance. *Kevin's in there. And he's probably already turtle food.* Hardly a pleasant image, but she needed to prepare herself for the worst. That was the most likely scenario, after all, unless she wanted to give any credence at all to Simon's logic.

If Simon's right, then this whole thing is going to end with me giving Kevin a big damn kiss while something explodes for no reason nearby, and neither of us will be bothered to look at it. A tempting scenario, but unrealistic.

So all she needed to do now was blindly enter the underwater cave that almost certainly held a giant creature capable of eating her in one bite. She wished she could say this was the craziest thing she had ever done, but it wasn't. The flares seemed like good thinking now, though. She took one from her belt and lit it. It would make her a target, but probably not much more than if she went in fumbling blindly. This way, if something saw her, she would at least see it back before it killed her.

Cautiously, she swam into the cave, trying to remain hyper-alert for anything that might put her in danger. The flare didn't penetrate too far into the darkness, but it was enough to know that the cave system was deep, probably going far into the heart of the rock below the island. The marine biologist in her sensed something off about the cave, but it took her a few seconds to realize what. The cave appeared to be completely devoid of life. There were no fish swimming in here, no benthic organisms like sea stars or mollusks crawling on the floor, not even any of the prolific green algae that she had seen all over outside the cave.

Probably because something ate it all, Maria thought.

Actually, no. She realized that wasn't true the deeper she went. The main lava tube remained unnaturally smooth and devoid of life, but she began to see a few side tunnels, many of them too small even for Maria to fit through, that did have the occasional creature crawling around. Those had to be the areas that Call It George was too small to get in.

She felt a thrum in the water, like a percussion wave hitting her from something farther down the tunnel. No, not a percussion wave. Actual water pressure pushing her back.

Something was coming down the tunnel. Something large enough to take up the majority of the space and displace the water.

Call It George had to be coming.

She looked quickly behind her, gauging the distance between her and the entrance to see if she had enough time to get out. She wasn't sure that she did. When she looked forward again, she thought she could see something moving down there, something very large, but it wasn't quite close enough for the flare to illuminate it. It didn't appear to be moving too quickly. Maybe the light intruding on its domain confused it. Whatever the reason, Maria didn't want to make the assumption that it would stay that slow. She'd seen already how fast Call It George could move when it wanted to.

The side tunnels. There had to be one big enough for her to squeeze through. Even if it didn't lead anywhere, maybe it would be enough for her to hide in while the creature passed. As the water continued to push against her, she frantically swam to the nearest wall, looking for any nook or cranny big enough to take her.

Something moaned. Something big. It was almost like a hooting noise, somewhere between a massive bird chirp and a whale song. In all the time Maria had spent studying marine biology, she'd never heard anything remotely like it. When she heard it again it was louder, closer.

Maria looked back down the tunnel. She thought she saw something gleaming in the flare light. Eyes? Yes, she decided. Eyes. Very, very large eyes.

Her whole body wanted to freeze. She again remembered Teddy Bear coming for her. She remembered the way she had actually needed to ride the shark's dorsal fin, her life depending on her ability to not let go. Somewhere in her mind, a part of her whispered to just give in the impulse to stay put, to let the creature come from her, to have it release her from the cycle of mental anguish that had begun months ago in the Sea of Cortez. Who knows? Had the circumstances been different, she might have even given in. But a different image popped up in her mind— Kevin, not as she had seen him minutes ago as the Zodiac had folded over him, but him sitting by her bedside in the hospital, her right hand covered by both of his, his fingers gently stroking her skin as she cried herself to sleep over the loss of her leg.

Kevin had been that for her. No one else, not even her family, had been there as much as he was. Now, she needed to be that guiding, saving presence for him.

There. A tunnel curved off to the side near the top, its angle in the stone hiding it until she had turned almost all the way around. While it was smaller than the main tunnel, it still looked more likely to fit her, complete with scuba tank, than anything else she'd seen. The haunting chirp grew louder, but she didn't dare take the time to look down the tunnel and see the sound's maker. She kicked as hard as she could for the side tunnel, letting go of the flare in an effort to give her an extra limb with which to swim. She could have made better time if she dropped the harpoon gun as well, but if this didn't work, she had a feeling she might need it in short order.

Maria went into the side tunnel, the sides close enough that she bumped her scuba tank, but she fit. Behind her, the flare gave faint illumination as it dropped to the lava tube's floor.

Then the light vanished as something enormous blocked the side-tunnel's entrance.

She stopped, pressing her hands against either side of the tunnel to keep the ebb and flow of the water from slamming her around. She was breathing heavily, which was a no-no given her limited oxygen. Maria held herself there, trying to force her racing heart to calm down as she waited for the thing blocking the entrance below her to swim past.

It took her nearly half a minute before she realized that her visitor wasn't going anywhere.

Call It George is still there, she thought. *It's waiting for* me. *It knows I'm here.* She figured that, even without any light, she would know when it was gone by the suction of water as it passed, but that didn't happen. After a few more seconds of pulling courage up deep from her inner well, she let go of the wall with one hand and fumbled at her belt for another flare. She would have cursed, if she'd been able to open up her mouth, as one came off her belt and almost slipped through her fingers. She got a hold of it at the last moment, though, then ignited it to look down at whatever was blocking her way.

All she saw beneath her was a single, giant black eye.

She almost dropped the flare in shock. The creature convulsed and blinked at the sudden intrusion of light, and for several seconds, a massive, rough eyelid closed over it. Then, slowly, it opened it again, but only part way. If Maria were to assign human emotions to the creature, she would say it looked wary.

It didn't move, though. She just floated in the tunnel, looking down while Call It George stared up. They were stuck in the world's most uneven staring contest.

Maria suddenly remembered that she had a small camera strapped to her head. *Oh man, Merchant is going to loooooooove this. Assuming I actually get out of here.*

The bizarreness of the situation amused her for a moment before certain inconsistencies dawned on her. The eye below took almost the entire entrance of this side tunnel. But she could have sworn that Call It George hadn't been this big when she'd seen it take Kevin and Ted earlier. The scale wasn't right. Either her initial impressions of the creature had been mistaken, or...

Maria dreaded the other possibility, but she didn't want to

jump to conclusions. She needed more information, more data. And maybe she could start gathering it as soon as Call It George swam on.

The creature blinked a few times, probably deciding that Maria wasn't enough of a morsel to continue waiting for, and the eye slowly moved from view. Even as it moved, though, Maria again realized she'd miscalculated the thing's size. The rest of the head slid past, and then its neck… and more of its neck… and more…

When the movement of scaly flesh stopped, Maria's best guess said that she'd seen something like fifty or sixty feet worth of the creature. And there was still more down the tunnel. Not only that, but the creature still blocked her way out.

Call It George was huge, bigger than any living creature she had ever personally witnessed. And it wasn't letting her out.

She expected herself to panic, but a strange calm came over her. All that was human about her wanted to recoil in revulsion at something fully capable of gulping her down purely by accident. The marine biologist in her, though, could only think of one word, over and over, with nothing else possibly describing the creature below her.

Beautiful.

With that thought, she looked up at the lava tube around her. It appeared to go on and twist away into the darkness, going deeper into the island.

With down no longer an option, she went up.

16

There were a couple of times where Maria was concerned the tunnel was too narrow to accommodate her, but she managed to squeeze by each time. At each of these squeeze points, she noted that the black volcanic rock was slightly smoother than in others, similar but not quite the same to the way the main tunnel had been worn down. Something had been through here at some point, although the tunnel didn't look like anything used it much anymore. That only furthered her theory, but she still didn't want to commit to it.

The side tunnel didn't go for long before it opened up and, to Maria's amazement, came out on a cavern that wasn't completely underwater. She broke the surface and treaded water for a moment, trying to get her bearings. The flare she'd been using was on its last legs, so she let it go and pulled out another. There'd been four on the belt, so after this she only had one left. It meant she was running out of time to find any sign of Kevin, unless she wanted to continue by fumbling around in the darkness.

The flare didn't penetrate far into the gloom, although she got the impression that the cavern was huge. She also got the distinct impression that she wasn't in here alone. Somewhere out in the darkness, she heard the echo of something scaly or rough scraping again stone. It couldn't be Call It George. She'd left it back in the tunnel, unless…

Oh wow. She had a thought, but it was too mind-boggling to give any credence. What if Call It George was still back in the main tunnel, but *also* in here? What if the mutant turtle creature was *just that big*?

Tentatively, she removed her rebreather and tested the air. Immediately, she had to fight from choking on the rancid stench. She remembered how, two days again, she'd almost been pleased by the natural scent of animal guano permeating the air of Isla Niña. This odor was like that, except there was no way anyone would ever try saying there was something pleasant about it. Turtle shit, she assumed. And, if Call It George was as large as Maria now suspected, probably a massive amount of it. She imagined a steaming brown pile roughly the size of a house and nearly gagged.

After a few breaths to get used to the stench, though, she thought she could detect a few other things. For one, while the air still tasted stale, it was at least breathable. She felt like she could get enough oxygen. That meant that, somewhere on the island, a lava tube must pierce the surface and act as an air shaft. Good to know, in case anyone ever needed a way in that didn't require diving and then swimming past a sea monster. She also thought she could smell something like putrid meat. Probably Call It George's food, or at least whatever might be left of it.

As much as Maria didn't want to admit it, that was likely where she would find Kevin.

Doing her best to follow her nose, Maria gently paddled first one way and then the other. Already she felt like she was lost. The cavern was huge, and without anything to act as a landmark, she was pretty sure she wouldn't be able to find the side tunnel again. When it was time to beat a hasty retreat, she would have to find another way out.

This is stupid, Maria thought. *I'm not going to find anything this way.* She thought about it for a second, then called out. "Kevin?" She doubted that yelling into a huge cavern that housed a giant sea monster was the best idea she'd ever had, but she was running out of ideas and adrenaline. And her body, still not used to being in the water, was tiring out fast. She waited for a few seconds, half expecting the giant turtle head to lunge out of the darkness and snatch her from the water.

That never came. But for the briefest of moments, Maria thought she could hear a distinctly human moan.

"Kevin?" she said again, although not quite so loud this time. A heartbeat later, the moan came again. This time, she thought it might sound something like her name.

Maria swam in the direction of the sound, where she soon found rough and ragged rock beneath her feet. The water got so shallow that it was only up to her knees, which made movement surprising difficult. Not only was she still wearing her flippers, which were hardly the best thing to have on in shallow water, but her prosthetic simply wasn't designed for normal walking. It kept moving in unpredictable ways. No, actually not unpredictable at all. The way the joints kept snapping this way and that, it was like her fake leg was still trying to swim. If she got out of this, maybe there were some improvements she could have made.

Even with the flare, the occasional rocks jutting out of the water were pitch black. That was why it was so easy to see the thin piece of orange-colored material floating in the water nearby. She splashed toward it and picked it up to inspect it. A torn piece of the Zodiac. She had to be close.

"Kevin?" This time, she kept her voice to just above a whisper.

And she got an answer.

"Maria? ...here."

Kevin's voice was faint, and he was obviously in pain, but his words were clear. Taking more care not to splash and alert anything in the water that she was here, Maria followed his voice until she saw a much larger piece of the raft half submerged in the water, floating under a rough, dark overhang of rock. Although it was folded over on itself, the chunk of Zodiac was still at least the size of a man and, as she watched, it shifted slightly from the inside.

"Kevin?" she said again as she pulled away the torn fabric.

He looked surprisingly good, for someone who had been nearly eaten by a monster sea turtle. He lay in the water, the rebreather still near his mouth, but the scuba tank was practically crushed and a couple jagged pieces of the tank had torn gashes in the chest of his wetsuit. There was some bleeding there, but not nearly as much as there could have been. Maria had been right: the Zodiac had taken the worst of the attack.

His eyes were closed, though, and his breathing seemed shallow. "Kevin? Honey, speak to me."

He mumbled something.

"I couldn't hear that."

He said it again, louder but still too slurred to make out. She leaned in close and put her ear close to his mouth.

"I… said… did you have… a nice… swim?"

Maria backed away, looked at him incredulously, then fought not to laugh. "You bastard. Next time you want to help me overcome my fear of going back in the water, pick a less deadly way to teach me the lesson."

"Oh, trust me… not part of the plan… was just going to get you to a swimming pool and throw you in."

She gave him a playful smack in the arm as he struggled to sit in an upright position. He made a sound in return that was half-chuckle, half-grunt of pain.

"Are you okay?" Maria asked.

"Ribs?" he said, sounding unsure. "Ugh. Yeah. I think some broken ribs." He looked around in the flare light, only now registering their environment. "Where are we?"

"Lave tube caves under Isla Niña," Maria said. "Apparently, the home of Call It George."

"Oh." He tried to get to his feet, but his equilibrium was off and he splashed back into the water. Maria looked around nervously, certain that any moment now their noise would attract the cave's resident.

"Is that scuba tank still usable at all?" Maria asked.

"Uh, pretty sure no," he said.

"We're going to have a hard time getting out of here, then. I think there might be a way to the surface of the island, but I haven't seen it. The only way out that I know of for sure is underwater. And also occupied by a sea monster."

"So we don't care about using this term anymore? Sea monster?"

"It almost swallowed you. If the name fits, after all."

"What about your tank?" Kevin asked. "Still plenty of air?"

"Yeah, for the moment. Maybe we can switch off as we swim. You know, you have the rebreather for a few seconds, then me."

"Going to make for an awkward swim, but probably our only option." He got to his feet again. This time, he almost kept his balance, but as the ripples of water pushed against his legs, he started to topple again. He reached out and grabbed the overhang he had been under, and for a few seconds, that held him up.

Then he fell again. Not because his legs wouldn't support him, but because the overhang shifted, moving away from them.

That wasn't a rock overhang.

Both of them scrambled to back away as the "rock" shifted, moving up and down a little. Maria saw how the light from the flare had cast shadows on it, making the irregular dark surface look like stone. Now that it moved, though, she could recognize the irregularities not as cracks and fissures but as scales. Her eyes followed the "overhang" to where it connected to a "wall," a wall that was now throbbing with underlying musculature. She followed the wall up, up, all the way up to the ceiling, where it abruptly curved away.

The large overhang was in fact Call It George's atrophied flipper. The wall was Call It George itself. And the giant turtle's shell was…

She didn't see one covering the creature, but now that she had a true sense of the thing's scale, she understood. It didn't have one, but it was still apparently driven on some primal scale to feel like it needed one to hide in.

The lava tube she had come in through was its head hole, which meant that Call It George's shell was the island itself. For all intents and purposes, the massive sea turtle *was* Isla Niña.

And they were standing inside it.

"We need to get out of here. Now," Maria said.

Kevin, unable to take his gaze away from the wrinkled and pocked skin of the ungodly-huge creature, nodded in agreement. "Yeah. Maybe a good idea."

A harsh, angry-sounding keen echoed through the chamber. The flesh near the flipper bunched as the sound got closer. Call It George was pulling its head back into the cavern. It knew they were there, and it was coming for them.

"Where's your exit?" Kevin asked.

"Uh, I don't know." She looked back in the direction she had come, but as the light of the flare flickered and lowered, she saw that she was completely lost. There was water, there was darkness, and that was it. Any remaining indication of where she had come in was gone.

"Here." Maria handed Kevin the harpoon gun. "Watch my back while I try to find how I came in."

Kevin eyed the harpoon. "You know, under any other circumstances, I would be confident that this was enough. Now though? I don't think it is."

Maria didn't get any chance to dive back in the water and try to find the way out. Something loomed out of the darkness, flinching back slightly at the light before coming into full view.

Call It George. A sea turtle. Neither title inspired much awe or fear. Neither one gave the proper to credit to the massive, magnificent, and terrifying beast looking at them.

Its head, curved around toward them on its impossibly long neck that resembled those of the Galápagos saddleback tortoises, was clearly-tortoise like in origin, but there was no one species that Maria would have been able to identify as its closest relative. She could see aspects of green sea turtles, leatherback turtles, various tortoises, and snapping turtles. All of that would have been fascinating enough even if it weren't for the fact that the head alone was ten feet tall.

Yes, definitely looks like Gamera, Maria said. *And definitely bigger than the one that grabbed Kevin. There's more than one.*

For several seconds, she could have believed Call It George didn't mean them any harm. The way it held its head, Maria was tempted to say it looked more curious than anything else.

Then it opened its mouth, and Maria heard something she'd never thought of in her wildest imaginings: the piercing, grunting roar of a giant killer sea turtle.

It lunged at them.

Maria shoved Kevin aside as the gigantic open mouth hurtled toward them. They both fell flat in the water, but not before she felt the breeze of Call It George's head passing over them. She wasted no time floundering in the water, instead getting right up, pulling her knife from the sheath, and ramming it up into the turtle's neck. To something that size, the knife might as well have been nothing more than a thumbtack, but it was large enough for the creature to feel it. It jerked away, almost taking Maria's knife with it. She got a firm grip on the handle at the last moment, and as she yanked it out, hot blood spattered her face.

Hot blood. Interesting, the biologist in Maria thought, before it occurred to her that maybe she had more pressing things to worry about.

"Kevin, get up!" she yelled. "Run!"

"Where?"

"Hell if I know!"

He was up and splashing away before Maria herself could get her balance again. There was a pause in the noise, as though he were stopping and debating if he were leaving her behind. Thankfully that didn't last long. Maria could handle herself, even if she suspected that after this she might have a few more traumatic issues to tack onto her previous experiences.

No biggie, she thought. *Whatever doesn't kill me only makes me sing more lines from that stupid song before I stop freaking out.*

Call It George's head and neck swung upward into the darkness just as the flare sputtered out. Making sure that she kept her bearings in the dark as much as possible this time, Maria crouched down and grabbed her last flare with her free hand, but she didn't ignite it. This one needed to last as long as possible, and there was a possibility she could use the darkness to her advantage. Somewhere behind her, Kevin's splashing stopped. He said a low curse that she couldn't quite hear, but that was the last noise he made. She worried for a moment, then figured that if something had happened to him, the sounds would likely have been much worse, like the frantic splashes of someone drowning or the sickening crack of bones as the giant turtle crushed him in its mouth. For these few seconds, everything went quiet. Maria forced her breathing to calm down, knowing her survival over the next minute might rely on her being as quiet as possible. It seemed unlikely that the darkness would hide her for long, given that this was apparently Call It George's natural state. Its eyesight in the dark was probably pretty good.

Which she might actually be able to use to her advantage, she realized.

For several seconds, there was nothing. Then she felt a breeze on her skin, soft at first, but getting stronger and coming in regular intervals. Breathing. Call It George's head was nearby, probably sniffing her out.

Something bumped her hand in front of her.

There was no time to think. Maria turned her head away and ignited the flare. The sudden brightness hurt her eyes, even when she wasn't looking directly into the light. A loud, surprised grunt from the creature, though, told her that it was affected even more.

Without looking, Maria thrust her knife in a downward arc, hoping that she would just happen to hit something important. The knife squelched, digging deep into something soft and spraying a substance that felt like jelly all over Maria's hand. Call It George made a noise that could only be a scream of pain. The knife was yanked out of her hand, and she fell back into the water. Looking up from her position on her butt, she finally saw what she had done. The knife was sticking out of Call It George's eye. She'd hit it near the bottom, and a dark puss was flowing freely from the wound.

Before she could move, Call It George lunged downward at her, its razor-sharp beak open wide to rip her apart.

Then there was a harpoon sticking out of the roof of its mouth, protruding through its flesh and presumably into its brain. Call It George thrashed its head back and forth, hitting it on the roof of the cavern and against its own body. Kevin's hand gripped her by the shoulders and pulled her away as the head fell, causing a massive splash in the shallow water.

"Thank you," she said quietly.

"Thank you right back," he said.

Call It George's one good eye was facing both of them, and it blinked uncertainly in the light. Maria waited a few seconds to see if it would go for another attack, but it didn't appear to have the energy. Kevin had hit something vital. This massive creature was dying.

Maria got to her feet and took a step forward, her free hand held out to touch it.

"Maria, I don't think you should…"

"Shh. Can't you hear it?" Unexpectedly, she was unable to keep her voice from trembling. Although the giant turtle-thing was no longer making those terrifying roar and grunting noises, the sound now coming from deep in its throat was somehow so much more horrifying. It was a sound that transcended species, the sound of pain and fear.

Kevin came up behind her and put his own hand on the creature's skin. She'd been afraid she would have to explain herself to him, but he was apparently on the same page. Not a minute earlier, Call It George had been trying to eat them, to kill them. But there had been no malice, no hatred in the action. It had been following its nature. They had been following their own in trying to survive. The fact that they had won did not make them superior. They didn't have the right to crow about their achievement and treat it like a trophy. They'd simply been lucky.

By Maria's way of thinking, Call It George was not an enemy they had vanquished. It was instead a magnificent, beautiful animal whose survival had been at odds with their own. It deserved their respect. Maybe even a little of their sorrow.

A tear ran down Maria's cheek as she stroked Call It George's rough skin. She looked over and saw that Kevin was crying as well. Call It George hooted pitifully several times, then went quiet. Its one good eye half-closed, then stopped.

"It's gone," Maria said softly.

"She," Kevin corrected. "At least biologically."

Maria nodded. She'd already suspected as much. "How can you be sure?"

"Because I found something. This isn't over." He waved for her to follow him as he went back the way he had run in the dark. Maria followed, holding up the flare like a torch for both of them to see. Back beyond the enormous flipper, the water grew even shallower, leading up to a ledge of rock just over the water. No, not rock, Maria realized, at least not completely. The volcanic basalt might have formed the base, but it had been shored up with turtle guano and what might have been sea lion bones into a more or less circular shape.

Maria knew what she was looking at even before she saw the

contents. At about thirty feet wide, it was probably the largest turtle nest in existence.

She saw footprints and scuff marks in the side of the rough structure where Kevin had blindly run into it. There were a number of shattered, pale pieces of material strewn all over the inside. Next to these were two eggs, each one by itself almost as tall as Maria. The tops had been broken open, and there were scraps of turtle-like bone all around them. Something had eaten their contents.

Maria thought of the breeding habits of the Nazca booby somewhere on the islands above her. When boobies laid their eggs, they always laid two at a time. This was believed to have evolved so that the boobies would have a maximized chance of breeding, one egg acting as a failsafe in the event that the first egg was eaten or failed to hatch. But once the two eggs hatched, the harsh realities of life in the Galápagos would set in. There simply weren't enough resources for the parent boobies to take care of two chicks at once. The strain would kill them if they tried.

And so the Nazca booby chicks had evolved a strategy that would seem horrific to human eyes. The first chick that hatched would push the second chick out of the nest, letting it dry up and die in the harsh Equatorial sun.

That looked similar to what had happened here. The two eggs looked like they'd been broken open on the top by some outside force. But instead of the unprepared hatchlings getting tossed out of the nest, something had gnawed on them.

Maria looked around at the broken and crushed pieces of eggshell surrounding the two that had never hatched. Assuming all of Call It George's eggs were roughly the same size as the two remaining, there were enough shards here for…

"Three?" Kevin asked her.

Maria nodded. "I was just about to say the same thing."

This wasn't over. There were at least three more giant killer turtles out there.

17

Maria had half-expected the *Cameron* to no longer be there by the time the two of them hobbled to the edge of Isla Niña near where Mrs. Schmidt had originally disappeared. But the boat was there, and after they waved their arms at it for long enough, Maria finally saw a flurry of activity on the deck, culminating in them launching the remaining Zodiac.

It had already been some time in the late afternoon by the time Maria and Kevin had seen the sun again. The final flare had lasted for a little while longer before guttering out and leaving them in total darkness. There had been a lot of fumbling around, some bruised shins, and Kevin was pretty sure he had a few broken toes in addition to his ribs now, thanks to outcroppings in the water he'd found the hard way. Maria had needed to whisper her mantra to herself for a while before she remembered her idea that there must be a lava tube coming out somewhere on the surface of the island. A long time of trial and error, along with some desperate and scared declarations of love in the dark between them just in case they didn't find the way out, eventually led to them feel the slightest of breezes flowing down from one of the tunnels.

Getting out had hardly been easy for a woman with one fake leg that wasn't designed for crawling around in caves and a man suffering from multiple injuries. There'd been a number of tense and scary moments. The tunnel had even gotten so thin that Maria had to ditch her tank to fit through. Eventually, the tunnel had brightened, though, making their diagonal climb easier, and broken the surface through a short cliff-face near the far side of the island. After what they'd just been through, climbing up the side felt easy, even as hungry and exhausted as they were. Then there'd been the final trek across the island to where the *Cameron* could see them. Under other circumstances, Maria would have been overjoyed at the prospect of walking uninhibited across one of the Galápagos Islands, but now she barely had the energy to stand, let alone examine her environment.

Cindy piloted the Zodiac that came to pick them up. The two of them quietly climbed (and almost fell several times) down into the raft while Cindy asked them a stream of questions that neither of them had the energy to answer. All Maria could manage was, "We'll explain back on the *Cameron*." Although Cindy looked disappointed at this, she grew quiet and dutifully piloted the Zodiac back.

While Cindy sat in the back controlling the motor, Maria and Kevin huddled together in each other's arms near the front. The buzz of the motor and splash of the water provided just enough audible cover that they felt comfortable having a private conversation, even with someone else with them.

"You going to be okay?" Kevin asked her.

"I think so," Maria said, then paused to gauge the truth of her answer. She was surprised to realize she wasn't lying at all. "I think I'm going to be okay."

"Are you sure? There were a couple times during the climb where I thought I might lose you. Mentally, I mean."

"I know, but really I think I'll be fine. Or, wait…" She reached down and yanked the flipper off her left foot. She held the foot up and wriggled her toes in the gentle sea breeze. "Now I'll be fine."

"I'm still not sure what to make of that. That really helps?"

"Bizarrely, yeah," she said. "Maybe that's a tic that's going to go away at some point. Or maybe the need to see my remaining toes and make sure they're there is going to be a permanent part of my personality for now on? Who knows? Think you can handle a girlfriend with a strange phobia for wearing a shoe?"

"Maria, I can handle anything at all with you. I take you however you come."

"Careful, I can make a dirty pun with that."

"Probably shouldn't," Cindy said. "I can still hear you both, you know."

"What about you?" Maria asked. "You going to be okay? I mean, I was only bitten by a shark. You were actually eaten. Sort of."

"Don't know. We'll see. Honestly, though, if I can survive

what happened to me in the bar, everything else is just gravy."

She didn't have to ask which bar he was talking about. She remembered it all perfectly.

The Zodiac made it back to the *Cameron* in record time, and the rest of the crew gently helped them both aboard. Kevin ordered Gutierrez to immediately head back to Puerto Ayora. Not only did he really need a doctor about now, but they had plenty to warn the locals about.

Maria sat down on the deck and removed her specialized prosthetic. Overall, she'd been happy with its performance in the water, although everything afterward had left much to be desired. She'd have to talk to the people who made it for her and have them tweak the design.

It'll be Bionic Leg Mark II, she thought. *Kind of like Iron Man. Holy shit, am I Iron Man now?* The idea made her strangely giddy. Kevin found a spot on the deck to lay down and rest while Maria attached her normal prosthetic. Everyone who wasn't doing something essential for the boat gathered around them.

"So?" Merchant asked. "What happened?"

"Here." Maria handed her the GoPro that had been strapped to her head. "See for yourself. I'm not sure what it all caught, but if it recorded even a fraction of what we saw, I can guarantee you huge ratings on *Sea Avenger*'s premiere episode."

Merchant looked like she was ready to salivate as she took the small camera in hand, but to Maria's surprise, she didn't immediately go check to see what it had captured. "But what about you?" she asked. "Are you going to be, you know, okay? You know, from now on?"

"Merchant, if I didn't know any better, I'd almost say you cared."

"I told you from the beginning that I'm not Vandergraf. If we're going to continue working together, you're going to need to learn to believe that."

"Maybe I will. I'm fine right now. Baby steps. Let's take a break before the next sea monster, though, okay?"

Even as the words left her mouth, she realized how badly she was jinxing them. Simon, who hadn't said anything so far, noticeably gasped.

"Yeah, um sorry about that. So, there's a couple things everyone needs to know. First, Call It George is dead. Second, Call It George was a female. She had babies. At least three."

They all stood and listened raptly as she recounted everything that had happened from the moment she had gone in the water to the point where they had emerged on the far side of Isla Niña.

"That's perfect," Simon chimed in when she was done. "If the mother was named Call It George, then the three babies can only be…"

"Simon, for God's sake, don't," Cindy said. Simon continued as though she hadn't said anything.

"…Hug It, Pet It, and Squeeze It!"

Whether they were too tired or because they knew it was pointless to resist, everyone just nodded as though those were perfectly acceptable names for baby gigantic sea turtles.

"They shouldn't be anything to worry about though, right?" Gary asked. He'd been so caught up in Maria's story that he'd forgotten to film her, although Charlene looked like she'd been picking up the slack. "I mean, their mother was a giant mutant, but babies should be easy to deal with, right?"

"Uh, no," Maria said. "Sorry to break it to you, but I think we've already seen the babies, or at least one of them. Call It George was huge. You should see it on the footage, but she wasn't the same creature that snatched up Kevin and Ted."

Ted, who'd been hanging back from the rest as though he was afraid just being around them would result in something trying to eat him again, spoke up in what could only be described as the frightened squeak of a hamster running from an owl. "You mean the thing that tried to kill me was the *small* one?"

"Yep. And unlike Call It George, who seemed to be grown into the cave like it was her shell, the babies probably aren't confined to one spot. That one that got Kevin and Ted didn't come from the direction of the island, remember."

"So what does that mean?" Merchant asked.

"It means we've got to warn people," Maria said. "At the very least, Isla Niña has to be shut down to visitors permanently. It's now the home of the world's only known species of gigantic sea turtle, and we already know they don't have any problem with seeing humans as food."

"You're going to just let them go?" Gary asked.

"We're not in the profession of eliminating endangered species just because they're inconvenient," Maria said.

Kevin moaned from his spot. "We still can't be sure that these giant turtles are naturally occurring, though."

"How could they not be?" Cindy asked. "It's not like someone one day just said 'Hey, you know what would be a fun thing to do over the weekend? Splicing together a bunch of turtle DNA and then mutating it. It'll be a blast!'"

"Sounds like a great weekend to me," Simon said. "Almost as fun as teaching the mutant turtles ninjitsu."

"You didn't see Call It George up close like I did," Maria said. "She definitely had traits from a number of different turtle species. I'd put more money on someone having engineered her than her occurring naturally."

"Especially since we've never seen anything like her before," Kevin said. "The Galápagos Islands may generally be considered remote, but in the modern world nothing is that remote. We would have found some hint of her species before. Anything from nests to bones in the fossil record. Something like that doesn't just spontaneously appear in nature. It would defy everything the islands themselves have taught us about natural selection."

"Still, I don't know if I can successfully spin that," Merchant said. "It's going to be interesting enough to try convincing people that whatever footage you got was real. No one's going to believe that someone genetically engineered Call It George on purpose."

"I would," Simon said. "Sounds like a great monster of the week to me."

"You don't count," Cindy said.

"Then don't say anything about that yet," Maria said. "On the unlikely possibility that this idea is true, we don't want people to get in a panic at the idea of someone creating giant sea creatures for shits and giggles."

"We'll need to say something to the authorities," Kevin said.

Maria nodded, although she wasn't sure she agreed with that. Without any clue about how this had happened, they couldn't be sure who to trust. The only guaranteed trustworthy people were those that were on this boat.

"We keep our suspicions to ourselves for now. Once we get back to the mainland, we can send a more qualified scientific team to study Call It George's remains. From there, whatever they find, that's what we'll go to the authorities with. Can everyone agree to that?"

Before everyone could voice their opinion, Gutierrez called to her from the cabin. "Maria or Kevin! One of you get in here!"

"Don't try moving, baby," Maria said to Kevin. "You just rest. I'll take care of this."

"Good idea. I'll just lay here and count my broken bones."

"If you really want to pass the time, make a song out of it," Maria said. "Works for me." She made sure her normal prosthetic was strapped on tight, then got back to her feet with Merchant's help and went to the bridge.

Gutierrez was at the controls, pushing the *Cameron* down around Isla Santa Cruz now at a speed that was probably illegal in these waters. He had the handset for their radio in his hand, and once he saw her, handed it over.

"It's that Padilla kid. Says it's important."

Maria took the handset. "Ernesto?"

It crackled in response. "Where have you people been? I've been trying to reach you for hours. I was getting ready to get on my boat and organize a search party."

"We're fine. Ish. We're not dead, at least."

"Excuse me?"

"Never mind. We can fill you in when we get back. In the meantime, you might want to let anyone in charge know that Isla Niña is probably going to be closed off indefinitely."

"You found it? Call It George was really there?"

"And then some."

"Well, me telling the mayor that no one can go out to Isla Niña probably will not go over very well. That's why I've been trying to radio you."

"What have you got, Ernesto?"

"I found out some information about what's been going on at Isla Niña prior to it being opened to the public."

Maria paused, thinking about everything they had just said regarding someone or something bigger involved in all of this. "Maybe this isn't something we should be discussing on an open band."

Ernesto paused. When he spoke again, he sounded embarrassed. "I'm sorry. I've already been using an open band to get most of this. I didn't think."

Maria sighed. "That's alright. Can't be helped. Tell me what you've got."

"I talked to someone with contacts in the Ecuadorian Navy. They're the ones who are supposed to be in charge of patrolling these waters and making sure no one violates the protected areas."

"Didn't you say they're pretty bad at doing that?"

"Oftentimes. Lots of corruption. But I was specifically looking for any corruption regarding Isla Niña."

"Okay. Continue."

"Apparently, around a year ago, a large sum of money crossed the palms of certain important people. The result was that for several months, the Navy studiously patrolled the area *around* Isla Niña without letting anyone go anywhere near it."

"Like they were acting as security for something that was happening there."

"Yes. Then, several months after that was over, Mayor Estevez suddenly became very interested in opening Isla Niña up to the public. He'd never seemed to care much about the island before, but all of a sudden, the addition of a new island to the itineraries was essential to the tourism trade."

"And let me guess: certain officials opened it up with no trouble."

"Yes."

Maria paused, trying to put all this together. It looked more and more like Call It George had not been a naturally occurring creature, or at the very least had been put here on purpose. And then what? The island had been specifically opened up so someone would discover it? Why go to the trouble of genetically engineering a creature in secret, if that was indeed what had happened, only to ensure that it was found?

"Do you know anything about the money trail?" Maria asked.

"It's not like under-the-table bribes leave a lot of paperwork."

"Right." So who would have done this? Was this a terrorist thing? Seemed highly unlikely. Genetic engineering of giant monsters was hardly the style of groups like the Taliban and ISIS. It had to be someone or some group with lots of money. How much money would that even take?

A thought suddenly occurred to her. Probably the same amount of money needed to hire a special ship to come out to the Sea of Cortez and try to tie up loose ends like Laramie.

Mercer, Maria thought, reverting back to the name she had originally known the young woman as, *what was it you knew that no one else wanted you to say?*

"Any physical evidence you have, I'll need it," Maria said. "Private channels in the future, though. Something smells incredibly fishy."

"That's probably because you're on the ocean."

Maria smiled. "Leave the bad attempts at humor to Simon. We'll see you when we get in. At this speed, it will probably only be a few more minutes. And try to get the mayor to listen!"

"I will try."

Maria handed the handset back to Gutierrez. For several long seconds, he gave her a funny look.

"What?" Maria asked.

"Are we in the middle of some kind of conspiracy?"

"Conspiracy's a strong word."

"I'm also betting it's the right word."

"Let's not jump to any conclusions. But in the meantime, everything you just heard doesn't leave the *Cameron*. I'm starting to feel a healthy sense of paranoia."

"Maria! Get out here!" Kevin screamed from out on the deck. She immediately turned and did her best impersonation of a run to join the others.

"What is it?"

"We've got a problem. A big one," Cindy said. She pointed out at the water behind them.

Ahead of them, they were just coming up around Isla Santa Cruz to the point where they could see Puerto Ayora, yet no one seemed to care about that view. Instead, every single person was looking in the *Cameron*'s wake as it sped through the water. At first, the churning water in the wake hid what had everyone's attention, but it didn't stay that way for long. Somewhere behind them, the water frothed more than it should simply from the *Cameron*'s presence. Something huge breached, then fell back to the sea before anyone could get a clear look at it.

"Hug It," Simon said reverently.

They'd been followed from Isla Niña. And now, thanks to them, Hug It was headed directly to Puerto Ayora.

18

"We've got to turn around!" Maria yelled into Gutierrez.

"What? Why?"

"Just do it! We can't let that thing near Puerto Ayora!"

"What? What the crap? What thing?" The *Cameron* shifted beneath them, though, as he gently led the boat away from the most populated area of the Galápagos Islands.

Behind them, some distance away yet closing in on them, Hug It raised its head on it long neck up above the water. It made a hooting, roaring cry that sounded similar to its mother, although this noise somehow managed to sound angrier. It splashed back below the water, and it occurred to Maria that, without an island to act as a sort of shell like with Call It George, as well as Hug It's long neck compared to its smaller body and fins that hadn't atrophied as much as it mother's, the creature looked remarkably similar to a plesiosaur. Was that just a coincidence, or had whomever or whatever had created the giant turtles done this in a specific attempt to recreate the prehistoric beasts? Maria supposed the question didn't matter much. Intention meant nothing here, only result. And the result looked like it was still pursuing them.

"Dear God, how can it move that fast?" Merchant asked. No one had their cameras up at this point, and Merchant was apparently too gobsmacked to order them to do otherwise. "I thought this thing was supposed to be a turtle."

"It might have started out as something like a turtle or tortoise, but it's not anymore," Maria said. "If these things were created by someone, we have no idea what abilities they spliced into it."

"It's beautiful!" Simon said.

"Bet you it won't look so beautiful from inside its stomach," Cindy said.

"How would you know?" he responded. "Have you ever been inside a sea monster's stomach? I hear they're quite nice this time of year."

"Banter later, survival now!" Maria yelled. "Everyone, get everything you can that's even slightly weapon-like."

The beast came up again, so much closer this time. Something seemed wrong about the way it moved when it dived back down, though.

"Yeah, uh, does this remind anyone of a previous moment?" Simon said. "Maybe we should start carrying weapons on the *Cameron* from now on."

Maria was about to tell him it was stupid to expect a sea-going science vessel to carry anything more potent than harpoon guns, but Kevin surprised her. "Yeah, I've got that covered. Monica, go grab the crate in the storeroom that's labeled 'fish sticks.'"

"Uh, fish sticks?" Monica asked.

"Just do it. Trust me." Kevin turned to Maria. "Even though we never expected what happened in the Sea of Cortez to happen again, I couldn't help but think we needed to be prepared."

"Guns?" Maria asked. "Did you bring guns? Holy shit, Kevin, you know how fricking illegal that is to be transporting guns in foreign waters!"

"Relax. Tranquilizer guns only. All the legal paperwork taken care of. What, did you expect me to be carrying semi-automatic assault rifles or something?"

Another splash from behind them. Maria missed seeing it as she was looking at Kevin, but she could clearly hear it. Strangely, it didn't seem to be getting closer anymore.

"Are tranq guns going to be enough against that?" Maria asked.

"Don't know," Kevin said. "We're probably about to find out. If we do manage to knock it out, we're going to need to act quickly if we don't want it to…"

"Hey, Kevin?" Cindy asked. "We've got a problem."

Everyone turned to look where she was pointing. Hug It breached again, but this time, it was no longer behind them. Still moving at the same speed, it had veered off away from the *Cameron*.

It was now headed straight for Puerto Ayora.

"Oh fuck!" Maria screamed.

"We're going to have to bleep that out," Merchant said absently. Charlene and Gary had both come to their senses enough aim their cameras at the action, but Merchant looked lost. Maria vaguely remembered that the woman's previous experience directing a reality show had been one of those weight loss shows, or something like that. Going from filming numbers on a scale to filming a sea monster about to attack a major human settlement was likely a shock to her system.

"Gutierrez!" Kevin said as he ran inside. "Back to Puerto Ayora!"

"Make up your mind!" Gutierrez hollered back.

"Just do it!" Kevin said.

Everyone had to fight to keep their footing as the boat shifted direction at unsafe speeds. Monica, who'd carried the fish sticks case up from below deck, stumbled and nearly lost the tranq guns over the side. Ted caught them in time, although "catching" might not have been the right word. It was more like the box smacked him directly in the face and bounced off. He fell to his knees with a bloody nose, but everyone was too frantic to take a closer look at him at the moment.

"Everyone who's not doing something, get those weapons loaded!" Maria screamed. She would have joined them, but given Hug It's speed, she was afraid to take her eyes away from it lest she lose it. Maria didn't want it to vanish below the water only to be next seen snacking on a tourist. And there was a smorgasbord waiting for it in the harbor. Most of the ships were at dock. The cruise liner with its brightly colored cartoon characters on the side, while not holding any tourists, was still noticeably swarming with maintenance workers prepping it for the next tourist wave. A small crowd had begun to congregate on the docks, most of them appearing to stare out at the *Cameron* as it moved toward them at speeds everyone knew were illegal. There was a Navy ship nearby, and it looked like the *Cameron*'s unusual activity had attracted their notice, as it was slowly starting to move in their direction. No one among them all seemed to notice yet that there was a swell in the water as something huge came right for them.

"We've got to do something to warn them," Maria said, more

to herself than anyone else, but what could she do? She could try contacting the Navy ship on the radio, but by the time she got anyone to listen, Hug It would already be coming out of the water and snatching people off the docks. There had to be something quicker…

"Flare gun!" Maria yelled. "Someone get me a flare gun!"

"Um, over here!" Simon said. She looked in his direction and saw him pulling one out of an emergency compartment. Maria grabbed it, ran back to the railing, and aimed at the dock.

Please don't hit anyone, she thought.

They were still far enough out that Maria couldn't be at all sure of her aim, but she had to take the chance. She pulled the trigger, and the burning flare launched out at the docks. It fell short, hitting the water not far away, but it still managed to do its job. The people in the harbor saw someone firing at them for no apparent reason and immediately began running back for land. The Navy ship must have seen it too, because she could faintly hear someone screaming through a bullhorn in Spanish that if they did not cease hostilities they would open fire. Maria only had a brief moment to worry that everyone on the *Cameron* was about to get shot.

Then Hug It shot out of the water.

The beast was probably the same one that had attacked Kevin and Ted, judging from its size. While that made it significantly smaller than Call It George, none of the people in Puerto Ayora knew they were only seeing the baby. All they saw was a sea monster out of their nightmares rising up for them, enormous dark eyes and a beaked snout at the end of a long, scaly neck. Anyone who hadn't already been screaming from the flare attack started screaming now, but the mad rush at least cleared the docks of Hug It's most obvious targets.

The Navy ship, which was now on just the other side of Hug It from the *Cameron*, erupted with gunfire. Most of the bullets missed, impacting the water. A few hit the creature, but just a few shots were little more than an annoyance to something that size.

"Tranq guns, now, or they'll kill it!" Maria said.

"But wouldn't it be better if they did?" Gary asked.

"We'll discuss the ethics of annihilating new species later, just start pumping that thing with tranquilizers!"

The *Cameron* came to an abrupt stop just out of the Navy ship's line of fire, but close enough that Maria could see the individual patterns of black and green on Hug It's back. Cindy and Monica came up beside her and started shooting, but Maria could already see there was no longer any point. Every single person on the Navy vessel had lined up along the side now, and each one fired whatever weapon they had right into the creature. Hug It screeched, a noise now filled less with rage than with fear, while the water around it turned red with its blood.

"Oh God," Maria said, unprepared for how horrified she was at the creature's fate. It was dangerous, true, but just like its mother, it was a living thing going according to the directives hard-coded into its genes. Now this magnificent animal was getting ripped apart by bullet-fire, patches of its skin exploding as the burst of bullets tore out chunks of meat.

"Stop," Maria said to the others on the *Cameron*. They all lowered the tranquilizer guns, each of them just as aware as Maria that any attempt to take Hug It alive was now pointless.

Hug It screeched as parts of its face erupted in blood. Then, with one last feeble cry, its head and neck crashed down onto the nearest dock. Even as it bled all over the wood, the Navy continued firing until the creature went completely still. The only movement was the occasional jerk from one of the last bullets hitting its neck, and the weight of its body trying to pull the rest of the carcass into the water.

The firing stopped. Everyone on the *Cameron* stood silently looking at Hug It's remains. The cameras, Maria noticed, were still filming.

After several moments of silence from both ships, a voice came over the bullhorn again. It started out speaking in Spanish, but after a few words seemed to realize the crew of the *Cameron* would better understand English.

"Do not move! By order of the Ecuadorian Navy, you are not to move your ship. We will send someone to board you. If you disobey these orders, we will open fire."

"God damn it," Maria said under her breath, but at least this was over. They would simply have to explain everything to whoever was in charge on that boat, and then they could declare their entire Galápagos adventure at an end.

"Maria?" Gutierrez called from inside. "Padilla's on the radio again. You need to hear this."

"Damn writer," Simon mumbled. "Can't let us have a moment's peace before the final climax."

"Brother, please shut up forever," Cindy said.

Being sure to move slowly so that no one on the Navy ship thought she was trying to make a break for it and shot her, Maria went inside and again took the radio handset. "Ernesto? Now's really not a good time."

"You are right. It's not. And your time is about to get worse."

"What is it?"

"It's Mayor Estevez. Right when I was trying to tell him that Isla Niña needed to be shut off from the public permanently, that creature attacks. We could both see it from where we were standing. He started babbling about fixing his mistake and ran off."

From the window of the bridge, Maria could sure a flurry of movement in the harbor. She grabbed the nearest pair of binoculars to see a number of men, one of whom might have been the mayor, running for some of the boats. They couldn't run that fast, though, as each of them was lugging some heavy container.

"I can see him now," Maria said. "Although I don't have the slightest clue what he and his people think they're doing. They're carrying something, but I can't tell what."

"I already know. I tried to stop them, but one of his thugs held a gun on me. Maria, those canisters are full of gas. The mayor is going to burn Isla Niña."

19

"Gutierrez, how much fuel does the *Cameron* have left?" Maria asked.

"Maria, we need to fill up before we can think about—"

"Just tell me how much."

The man looked at her grimly, but there was nothing about his voice that sounded challenging. Gutierrez would follow along with whatever she decided. "We have enough to get back to Isla Niña. Maybe enough to return after that, but I doubt it."

"Good enough for now," Maria said to him, then turned her attention back to the handset. "Ernesto, I'm assuming no one's pointing a weapon at you now if you're making this call?"

"No. Estevez's man left to help him load the gas."

"Right. See if there's anything at all you can do to stall them, but don't put yourself in danger. You've already done so much."

"I'll see what I can do."

Maria handed the binoculars to Gutierrez. "Keep an eye on the mayor. Make sure I know if they leave. And be prepared to take off after them if I tell you."

"What about the Navy?"

"Let me see what I can do. But just in case I fail, that ship looks big and heavy. Hopefully, the *Cameron* is faster."

"I should have known when I woke up this morning that I was going to get shot at," Gutierrez mumbled.

"At least nothing has tried to eat you today, which puts you ahead of several people standing on this boat."

"That's true, I suppose. Got to appreciate the little things in life."

Maria flagged down Kevin and told him what she knew, along with a rough idea of what she had planned. Although she had expected him to protest, he just nodded and said he would support whatever she decided. While he went to quietly inform the others what might be about to happen, hopefully without arousing the suspicion of anyone on the Navy ship, Maria turned her attention back to the radio and tried to find a channel to reach the captain of the ship.

She finally got someone on the ship, but he refused to put her through to the captain. As she argued with the Navy equivalent of middle-management, Gutierrez grunted.

"Looks like they're all loaded up."

"El capitan esta comiendo no debe de estar estorbado," the radioman said.

"Mierda que esta comiendo! Si tomaria su trabajo de proteger estas isla's enserio, se reportaria por radio y esuchar lo que tengo que decir!" Maria looked to Gutierrez. "I'm not getting anywhere with this guy. I hope you know how to patch bullet holes in the *Cameron*."

"Is this going to be common thing from now on? Should I get some kind of insurance against accidentally being shot in the head?"

"Don't worry. This will be the last time something like this happens, I swear."

"Are you lying?"

"Probably."

"Looks like they're taking off. Three small boats. They'll probably be hard to catch with something the size of the *Cameron*."

"Then I guess we don't have any more time to waste," she said. She turned off the radio. "Time to try something else. Ready to put the pedal to the metal?"

"The *Cameron* doesn't have a pedal."

"Smartass." She went back out on deck. Up on the Navy ship, the crew had lowered most of their weapons, obviously not expecting the *Cameron* to be any more of a threat. Every single person on the *Cameron*, however, had either gone below deck or were now sitting against something that would keep them from flying off the boat if it suddenly started moving. Which was exactly what it was about to do.

Maria watched one of the sailors turn around so he could light a cigarette and hide the flame from the wind. Several of the others were chatting. One still had his weapon ready but wasn't looking at them, instead watching a storm petrel as the bird flitted overhead.

Maria leaned back into the cabin and braced herself in the doorway. "Now!"

The *Cameron* was a modified trimaran yacht. It wasn't designed for sudden acceleration, especially when they weren't even facing the direction they wanted to go. Yet Gutierrez knew it, and he knew had to coax things from the boat that someone new to it would have thought impossible. With a lurch, the *Cameron* started up and whipped in a tight, fast circle. Anything on the bridge that hadn't been strapped down flew across the room. Maria, again forgetting that she didn't have the same balance that she used to, slammed into the wall but just barely managed to keep from falling. For several seconds, there was no gunfire, and Maria hoped they'd somehow managed to catch every single sailor on deck off guard, before she heard a couple of pops in the air. Nothing seemed to hit the *Cameron*, though, and as the boat faced a hundred and eighty degrees from its original position, she saw everyone onboard the Navy ship scrambling, some trying to line up a shot and others preparing for the ship to take evasive maneuvers. Their ship was now the one facing the wrong way, though, and Maria doubts they could turn it around with the same speed.

"Good! Go, go, go!" Maria yelled at Gutierrez.

"No, I think maybe I'll just stop right now while we're being shot at. Of course I'm going. You and your man have hired me to do this job, so just shut the hell up and let me do it!"

Deciding it was probably best to stay out of his way from this point on, Maria left Gutierrez and staggered onto the deck to join the others. Although everyone was still bracing themselves against the boat's speed, they all had a grim and determined look as they gathered together.

"Look, we're now in the realm of doing something illegal," Maria said. "At the very least, the Ecuadorian Navy has us for resisting them. At most, we might get charged with other crimes against the mayor if we try to stop him."

"But isn't what he's doing illegal?" Ted asked. Or at least that was what she thought he asked. Between his broken nose, the blood running down his face and into his mouth, and the rasp he still had from getting a lungful of seawater, he was almost unintelligible.

"Oh, most definitely," Kevin said. "He's about to deliberately destroy part of a protected World Heritage Site. No matter how powerful he thinks he is or how high up his friends might be, he'll get called to task for this. But we can't let him actually go through with it, and the legal morass this is sticking us in is going to follow us for a long time."

"So anyone who wants to claim that they're not a part of this, speak up now," Maria said. "No questions from us, no retribution. I and Kevin, and everyone else on this boat, I hope, will say to the authorities that these people had nothing to do with our decision, tried to stop us, and were held against their will."

"Wouldn't that just put another charge on you guys?" Gary asked.

"Probably. But this is your last chance to be an objector and possibly get out of any legal ramifications."

Without even speaking, Monica moved next to Kevin and Maria. After a few seconds, both of the Gutsdorfs joined her. That left only the television crew.

Merchant looked around at her people, then at Maria. "You realize there's legalese in your contracts that say the network can sack you for any illegal activity?"

"Yes. Of course, if the network were to happen to get footage of me stopping someone from destroying a World Heritage Site…"

"Okay, you can stop. No need to appeal to the producer in me. I just wanted to make sure you knew. I've come this far with you, so I'm certainly not going to stop now."

One by one, every single person in the TV crew gave their consent.

The three smaller boats had a head start, and soon they lost view of them. The Navy ship behind them was also falling behind, though, so there was still a chance they could do something. By the time Isla Niña came into view again, every person not carrying some kind of television equipment was armed with one of the tranquilizer guns, even Merchant. As soon as the island poked over the horizon, Kevin had his binoculars out and was scanning the island for Estevez and his people.

"Well?" Maria asked, standing beside him. The light was fading again, reminding her of the night one of the turtles had shown itself to them for the first time and sent her into some kind of fit. She thought she could deal with it now if either Pet It or Squeeze It showed up, or at least she could keep her cool in the moment. Once this day was over, she planned on crawling into bed next to Kevin and not poking her head back above deck until they were back on the mainland. The Galápagos Archipelago might still be the land of her dreams, but a vacation it was not.

"Their boats are already there, but it doesn't look like they picked a particularly good place to land. Estevez obviously doesn't come out here that often. They're having a hard time lugging the gas cans up the rock face, I think."

"How many people?" Maria asked.

"Looks like four. Estevez is already up on the island. Seems to be barking orders at the others. We might still have time to stop them, we might not."

"This is the dry season," Maria said. "They probably don't even need all that gas. Just a little accelerant and a match, and the whole island could go up."

"What does he even think this will accomplish?" Monica asked. "Pet It and Squeeze It are in the water."

"Maybe he's not that smart," Kevin said, sneering. "It's not like he impressed me that much."

"Or he could be trying to destroy some evidence," Simon said.

Cindy raised an eyebrow at him. "What do you mean?"

"Maybe there's something on the island that gives a clue where Call It George and her babies came from," Simon said. "And if he knows about it…"

"Maybe," Maria said. "I suppose we're going to have to ask him. After he wakes up from all the tranquilizers we're going to put in him. Monica, make sure the Zodiac's ready."

"Do we really need to follow the rules about keeping a larger boat away from the island at this point?" Charlene asked.

"The rule isn't just there to protect the species of the island, it's there to protect us as well," Maria said. "Too many shallow rocks and coral reefs. Even something the size of the *Cameron* would be too big to avoid getting torn up."

"With only one Zodiac at the moment, that means, at best, that we can have three or four people going to the island," Kevin said.

"And we should probably leave at least one in the Zodiac to pilot it around in case of an emergency."

"Want to draw straws to see which one of us goes?" Kevin asked.

"Hell no. You're not going."

"But…"

"But you have broken ribs, broken toes, and broken who knows what else. Forget about all of that? The last thing we need is for one of those guys to hit you and send a rib into your lungs."

Kevin sighed. "I'll stay behind on the *Cameron*. I'll have Gutierrez take it as close as is safe, and all of us that stay behind will try to use the guns to cover you."

"So I'm going," Maria said. "Who else?"

Both Simon and Cindy volunteered, with Simon being designated as the one who would stay in the Zodiac and keep it ready for a quick escape if needed. After a little back and forth, they finally decided that Gary and his camera would be the fourth. He wouldn't be able to get out and help Maria and Cindy on the island, but they figured it would be good to have a visual record of anything that happened to use as evidence in their favor when the Navy got them.

As they got close enough to launch the Zodiac, Kevin looked through the binoculars again for an update. "Looks like they've got all the gas cans off the boat."

"Pouring gas on the island will all by itself probably do irreversible ecological damage," Maria said.

"We may already be too late to stop that," Kevin said, "so let's see what we can do about keeping it from getting worse."

"Any sign of our two long-necked friends?"

"Honestly, we can't even be one hundred percent sure they exist at this point. Remember, we were only guessing how many based on the eggshell pieces. But no, not seeing anything. Be careful, though. Especially at that spot on the island where Mrs. Schmidt was taken. If they exist, then that's the place where they'll be."

"Duly noted. Okay everyone, saddle up!"

As the Zodiac launched, Maria risked a look back at the approaching Navy ship. It was still some distance away, but now that the *Cameron* had stopped, their time before the Navy's arrival would be short. Between keeping the mayor from burning Isla Niña and having their pursuers catch up, their time to do this was limited.

Simon expertly sped the Zodiac right up to the place where they had tied off on their earlier trip, and Maria and Cindy, both carrying their own tranquilizer rifles, went up the side of the island. Maybe it was the adrenaline, or maybe it was the idea of a ticking timer before everything went irreversibly to hell, but Maria didn't have the same trouble climbing the rocks that she had the first time. Or maybe she was just getting used to this.

This is my life now, Maria thought as she twisted her prosthetic leg to keep it from getting caught on the basalt. *This is my life and I can do it.*

Once they were both up, Simon drove the Zodiac a slight distance out, trying to get into a position where he could see them both. Gary's camera, Maria noticed, stayed on her the whole time.

"Over there," Cindy said, pointing to where they had seen the mayor and his cronies unloading their deadly cargo. As they ran in that direction, Maria noticed that the four men had already started their damage. Several booby nests had already been trampled, and several iguanas lay sprawled and broken nearby as though they had been kicked. On a nearby cactus, a small cactus finch tweeted shrilly at them, as though it understood what was going on and wanted them to hurry up and save it. The relatively flat terrain allowed Maria to see where they had piled the gas cans, and two of the mayor's men already had some open to pour on the ground.

"Stop!" Maria screamed at them. The mayor looked up,

appeared startled by their presence, and then said something to the one henchman without a gas can.

The guy pulled out a pistol and, without bothering to take careful aim, fired at them.

"Shit," Cindy said, skidding low on the ground to take up some poor cover behind a stunted tree. "This was not part of what I was expecting for today."

"Get in line," Maria said as she ducked low near a rock outcropping. The initial shots were nowhere near either of them, but they weren't in a very good position to return fire. Maria peeked around the outcropping to see that one of the men with a gas can was running away from them, dumping a steady stream of gas behind him in the water-starved vegetation. "We've got to…"

Before she could finish, Cindy jumped up from behind her cover and took aim with her tranquilizer gun. The guy was too far away, and the gun wasn't designed for that kind of long distance shot. Maria would have warned her that she didn't have a chance at making the shot, except Cindy was too quick.

Cindy pulled the trigger, and to Maria's surprise, the man staggered as a tranq dart hit him right in the neck. He dropped the gas can and staggered, but didn't immediately drop to the ground.

"Holy hell," Maria said. "How did you do that?"

"My grandpa taught Simon and me had to use guns when we were kids," she said. If this had been any other time, Maria would have questioned how that training translated to weapons that weren't intended for long-distance sniper shots, but the man with the gun fired at them again. Cindy ducked back down. Maria kept an eye on the man she had shot just long enough to see him drunkenly pull something out of his pocket. It was hard to be sure from this distance, but she thought it might be a lighter.

"No, no, no, we've got to stop him," Maria shouted. "If he…"

Even from so far away, she could clearly see the lighter spark up in the waning light. The man collapsed from the tranquilizer, but the lighter stayed lit as it fell into the grass.

That particular patch of vegetation hadn't received the same gasoline soaking as the parts behind the man, but the grass caught easily. A fire started next to the man's prone body, and anybody with half a brain could tell how quickly the fire was going to spread.

They had no way to put it out. They were too late.

The mayor and his two other men saw this and immediately began to panic. The other who had been holding a gas can dropped it and, despite the mayor's frantic pleas, ran back in the direction of their boats. The one with the gun ran in a completely different direction. Maria didn't think he would find anything to help him that way. He simply picked the direction that was most opposite the prematurely started fire and ran, dropping the gun behind him.

That left Mayor Estevez himself, who stood still and surveyed the sudden chaos around him, finally seeming to wonder what the hell he had done.

Then he, too, ran. Maria's mind flashed red with anger. She couldn't let him get away with this.

"Cindy, go see if you can rescue that guy you tranqed before the fire kills him," Maria said. "Then get him to their boats and escape."

"What about you?"

"Estevez is mine," she said, then picked up her tranquilizer gun and ran after him.

The air began to grow black, both with the coming night and the thick black smoke of the burning vegetation. Trying to run flat out with her prosthetic was awkward, but she was surprised how quickly she was learning to adapt. She passed the small pile of gas cans and saw Estevez getting closer to the edge of the island. Out on the water, she could see the Navy Ship coming up alongside the *Cameron*, where it slowed for a moment before coming closer to the island. They must have seen the fire, but given the ship's size, it would still be forced to keep its distance. If the ship had any way to put out the fire, it probably would be too little too late.

"Estevez, stop!" she yelled. The mayor came to a halt at the edge of the island. He looked down into the water as though considering jumping. Maria raised her tranquilizer gun. "Don't do it! I'll put a tranq in you and you'll drown. Just stop and come back with me.

"No, this isn't right. I messed up. I can't go back or they'll come for me," Estevez said.

Maria slowly stepped closer. Something about this part of the island looked familiar, and it made her uneasy. "Who will come for you? What's this all about, Estevez?"

"No one was supposed to die. They never told me anything about that. If they had, I wouldn't have taken their money, I swear!"

"Who? Whose money, Estevez?" She kept inching closer. The smoke grew thicker and choked off her air as she finally realized where they were. The Navy ship moved closer on the water, closer enough that she could hear shouting from the deck.

Maria thought she heard something moving in the water just over the side from Estevez.

"Paperclip Unlimited. That's the name they gave for the company," Estevez said. "They did this! They created that monster! I just wanted to destroy anything they'd done here, to protect the people. I swear I wouldn't have…"

"Apologize later, Estevez. For now, just come toward me. Away from the water, away from…"

Instead, Estevez took a step closer to the edge. He didn't seem to realize how close he was. He also couldn't possibly know that he was standing in exactly the same spot where Mrs. Schmidt had been taken.

"They said there was more," Estevez said. "They said their projects were everywhere. If they are all like this, then you have to…"

The water below Estevez erupted. The creature, Pet It, snapped Estevez in its jaws before the man could finish. Gunfire again sounded from the Navy ship, and Pet It screeched in pain even as it chomped down so hard on the mayor that the man snapped in half, his bloody torso flying one direction while his legs went the other. Bullets zinged by Maria's head. She turned and ran, knowing the Navy was aiming for the creature, not her, but suspecting they wouldn't care much if they hit her by accident.

Going back the direction she had come, Maria stopped short as she saw the conflagration that Isla Niña had become. The fire was spreading in all directions. There was no sign of Cindy or the man she had shot, but Maria had a clear view of the fire racing along the trail of gas the man had left behind.

It was heading straight for the pile of gas cans, most of which would still be full.

Maria dropped the tranq gun and quickly scanned her surroundings. The Navy was occupied with killing Pet It, just far enough away now that she didn't think she would get accidentally shot. She could see the edge of the island, and out beyond it there was Simon and Gary, Simon motoring closer to the island while Gary kept the camera squarely on her.

She risked a quick glance back at the fire and gas cans. Maria had seconds at most.

Running for the edge, a random memory came to her of the day she and Kevin had arrived in Ecuador. What was it he had said as they got out of the limo?

Remember, you're an action hero now. Walk towards the Cameron *as though there's an explosion behind you and you're too badass to look at it.*

As she leaped off the edge and dove for the water, the pile of gas cans went up behind her. She felt the heat of the explosion at her back. The last thing she saw as she plunged into the sea was Gary, a look of shock and awe on his face, as he filmed the whole thing.

20

Isla Niña burned late into the night.

As much as everyone wanted to go back to Puerto Ayora, there was far too much to deal with here. Maria's long hoped for crash into bed with Kevin didn't come until the late, late hours, considering she and everyone else were too busy being interrogated by members of the Ecuadorian Navy. More ships turned up in the hours following the deaths of Mayor Estevez and Pet In, whose charred carcass could be seen hanging off the edge of the island when the wind blew the fire just right to illuminate it. At least one of those ships, though, had carried representatives of the American consulate. Merchant had been able to use them to make a few key calls. The result seemed to be that no one on the *Cameron* was going to get arrested. That didn't mean the Navy went easy on them during the questioning.

By the time Maria finished all the questioning and was allowed to return to the *Cameron*, the first hints of morning light could be seen on the horizon. Many of those who had not been quite so neck deep in this mess had been allowed to return hours earlier, meaning that the only sound she could hear when she wearily climbed back aboard the boat were the occasion snores from the people sprawled in and on the *Cameron*, many of them just collapsed in a corner from exhaustion and falling asleep there. Even Kevin had apparently been returned half an hour earlier, and she assumed he was in bed, but despite her exhaustion, Maria couldn't bring herself to go down to join him yet. She felt like she was duty bound to watch Isla Niña's funeral pyre.

The *Cameron* had been moved farther away from the island to make room for the Navy blockade, which now surrounded the three-mile-wide island. There wasn't much they could do to put the fires out, but they could keep it from spreading. This was an ecological disaster, but it didn't need to do damage to the rest of the archipelago.

That didn't make this anymore heartbreaking.

As Maria leaned on the railing, staring up at the rising plume of black smoke that finally looked like it was petering out, she got the impression that someone was slowly coming up behind her. She braced herself, ready to fight if it was some attacker like one of the mayor's surviving men (even though all three of them were supposed to be in the brig on one of the Navy ships). More likely it would be Kevin, though, here to comfort her. That made it all the more surprising when instead Merchant came up and joined her at the railing.

"Is that going to cause a problem?" Merchant asked, pointing at the smoke. "I mean, an environmental one? For the other islands?"

"Possibly, but more because of any pollutants from the gas, I would think. Smoke itself is nothing new in the Galápagos. There's active volcanoes farther to the west, remember."

"Ah." Merchant pulled a tissue from somewhere and held it out to Maria.

"What's that for?"

"Your cheeks. You've been crying."

"I have?" Maria touched her fingers below her eyes. They came away wet. She took the tissue and wiped the tears away. "So much for me being the Indiana Jones of the sea."

"How do you figure?" Merchant asked.

"Indy doesn't cry when the temple he's raiding is destroyed around him."

"Maybe that's not the kind of hero we need anymore. Maybe we need one who's aware of the ramifications of their actions. Or one who needs time and help to deal with the horrors she's seen. I think people are ready for that, aren't you?"

Maria shrugged, but she had to admit that something about Merchant's words put her at ease. "The small cactus finch," Maria said quietly.

"Excuse me?"

"This small patch of land was the only place in the world where the small cactus finch could be found. One of Darwin's celebrated finches. Gone now. Extinct. Erased forever from the world. All because a corrupt, small-minded man couldn't think of a subtler way to solve his problems."

"Did he say anything to you on that island?" Merchant asked. "Before the creature got him?"

Maria hesitated. When the Navy people had asked, she'd told them everything that had happened over the past several days, all the way from their arrival to the moment she had jumped for Simon's Zodiac. Except, that was, for the things the mayor had said in his last moments. She had no idea who or what Paperclip Unlimited was, but she got the distinct impression that they were bad news. They were the ones that were responsible for this mess and, now that she thought about, probably for at least some of the things that had gone done in the Sea of Cortez. And whatever they were doing, Isla Niña couldn't be the end of it. There had to be more.

They'd been able to buy the mayor of Puerto Ayora. They had been able to pay the entire Ecuadorian Navy to look the other way, at least for a brief time. So where else might their influence be?

For now, she decided, she would keep the name Paperclip Unlimited to herself. Kevin could know, but no one else.

Maria shook her head. "No. Whatever secrets he knew about Call It George and her babies, he took them with him."

"You should probably know, that Padilla guy was trying to get a hold of you earlier. He knows what happened. Hell, most of the world will pretty soon. Some news outlets are probably on their way right now."

"Probably not that many, though," Maria said. "The average television viewer doesn't actually care that a number of rare animals have been destroyed. All they care about is which celebrity accidentally released a sex tape."

"Maybe you can fix that," Merchant said. "Isn't that why you wanted to do all this?"

"I wanted to do all this so I could pay for my medical bills."

"Oh come on, I know you and Kevin are more idealistic than that. And this is your chance. You can make people care that an irreplaceable part of the world was wiped out."

"Is that enough, though? We can try to tell people, but as long as there are still Mayor Estevez's in world, does anything we do or say help?"

"You know he's not mayor anymore, right? Kind of hard for someone in multiple pieces to take bribes."

Maria winced.

"Oh shit. I'm sorry. I wasn't thinking about you and your... you know." She gestured at Maria's leg.

"Don't worry about it."

"What I was trying to say is that the spot of mayor in Puerto Ayora is open. All that needs to happen is for the spot to be filled by a good person. Maybe a certain young man who knows the local tourist industry inside and out, yet still wants what's best for the islands?"

Maria looked at her, a smile slowly coming to her lips. "Ernesto would be pretty good for the job, wouldn't he?"

"I'm sure he can be convinced to run," Merchant said.

They both went quiet for a time as they watched the sun rise through the haze of smoke. "There's still a problem, you know," Merchant finally said.

Maria nodded. With all the excitement, she was wondering if anyone else would notice the one remaining loose thread.

"Are you sure that there were three hatched eggs down in that cavern?" Merchant asked.

"No, I'm not. Kevin and I were just guessing based on the broken pieces of eggshell we found. They were pretty shattered, it was dark, we were both tired and scared. We could have been wrong. Very easily."

"But do you think you were?"

Maria shrugged. "It's possible. Maybe even likely. Hug It, Pet It, and Call It George could have been all there was of our mutant turtle friends. Or Squeeze It could have existed after all, and it didn't survive as long as the others. The Galápagos is a harsh environment, after all."

"You didn't really answer the question, though. Do you think there's a third baby out there?"

"Probably because it's not a question I can answer. If you

forced me at gunpoint to make a guess? I suppose I would say I believe it's over. I think we've seen the last of them."

Merchant nodded, said goodbye, and went to find a place to sleep. Maria couldn't tell whether or not Merchant knew she was lying.

*

She fled.

She lacked the ability to make context of the turmoil taking place at the surface. All she had was her instincts telling her that something had gone wrong, that she had to go, that she must flee. Her mother was dead, one of her sisters was limp next to the island that had been their home, and her other sister had vanished. The water above her churned with too much activity, and the cavern that she had been born in was uncomfortably hot.

So she swam. She had no concept of how long it took her, but when she found an underwater cave, she instinctively took shelter there, feeling like it provided something she was lacking. Protection. A home.

The creature that had been dubbed Squeeze It finally calmed. She could stay here for a while. She could grow and thrive. And she could wait.

21

Maria brought the pies in from the kitchen and set them on the table. As soon as she'd seen Mama putting the pies in the oven, she'd known that tonight's dinner would be different from the last time. These pies weren't store-bought. They were homemade. Mama had spent hours making them with love.

Mama came up behind her with the plates, setting one in front of everyone. This time, Maria noticed there was no passive-aggressive placement for Kevin. His dish was as close as anyone else's.

This dinner had been so different from the last one that it was hard to believe she was even in the same house with the same family. To start with, there was no television crew. Maria had politely asked Merchant for them to have this time in private, just her and her family, and Merchant had relented. The executives at TEC weren't so desperate for footage anymore. Indeed, they'd gotten so much to work with in the Galápagos Islands that they could fill more than just one episode, and it was action-packed enough that they didn't need to manufacture any additional family drama. Indeed, a family spat would have looked boring and anticlimactic after the footage of Maria leaping off the exploding island.

Despite the environmental disaster it represented, Maria had no choice but to admit she'd been right: the footage really did make her look like the ultimate badass.

And there was no family spat for the crew to film, anyway. When they'd come in, Mama had hugged both her and Kevin in quick succession, all of the previous tension apparently gone. Papa was still a little stiff around Kevin, but he remained cordial. Ramon and Felix both joked around equally, often including Kevin in on the humor. It was an amazing turnaround. Maria wasn't quite sure what had caused it, but she wasn't going to question it for fear that it would all be revealed as a dream.

As Mama served the pies, though, Maria could no longer keep her curiosity to herself. "Okay, so can I finally ask what's going on?"

"Why, whatever do you mean, dear?" Mama said in a tone that clearly said she knew exactly what Maria was talking about.

"You're treating me and Kevin like, well…"

"Like family?" Felix asked.

"Yeah. Like that."

"Maria, don't be silly," Mama said. "You are family."

"Yes. I am. But Kevin…"

Everyone stopped and looked at Kevin. He'd remained fairly quiet through most of the dinner, probably because he was as confused about the sudden turnaround as Maria was. He looked uncomfortable under the sudden scrutiny, but then again, maybe that was because he was still in some amount of pain. The broken bones he'd received underneath Isla Niña were still healing, after all, and slower than they should have been. Although Maria had to admit that was probably partially her fault. With the camera crews no longer around so much, Maria had been taking advantage of their time alone. There were times when she might have been a little rougher than his body needed right now.

Papa took a deep breath and answered her. "Maria, Kevin is family, too."

The words weren't exactly a surprise, given the way they had been acting all night, but it still felt like a heavy weight was lifted from Maria's chest. "What happened to all that talk from before? About him being old enough to be Papa?"

Papa sighed. "I'm still uncomfortable with that."

"As am I," Felix said.

"Actually, you can thank Ramon," Mama said. "He's the one that wouldn't let up on us until we listened."

"Your friend Merchant showed me some of the early footage from the show at one point," Ramon said. "I saw the way Kevin was with you when you were recovering. And I made sure everyone else knew that I thought that was more important than his age."

"Look, Kevin, we're terribly sorry if we made you feel less

than welcome the first time you were here," Mama said to him. "We weren't thinking. All we wanted was what was best for our girl."

"Not a girl. A woman," Maria mumbled, but she didn't put much fight in the words. She understood the point Mama was trying to make.

"And I want what's best for her as well," Kevin said. "I love her. I would never intentionally do something to hurt her."

"And I love him, too," Maria said as she took Kevin's hand. "That should be enough."

"Oh, it is," Mama said, although there was something knowing in the way she said it that made Maria suspicious. Hoping Kevin's lesser grasp of Spanish kept him from understanding, Maria switched languages.

"Por que cambiaste tu mente, Mama? Que estas tratando de realizar?"

Mama smiled. "Ahi corazon, no hay otros motiros. Nomas quiero asegurarme que mi hija esta con un hombre que le de un orgasmo cuando la llenando de placer."

"Mama!" Maria said, shocked and really hoping now that Kevin hadn't understood that. Judging from the way he smiled and blushed, he'd understood enough.

Her brothers started laughing, which got Papa laughing, and soon everyone is the room was laughing. As it tapered off into congenial, good-natured small talk among everybody, Felix held up a finger.

"I almost forgot. Maria, you got something in the mail a couple days ago."

Maria frowned. "Really? I haven't lived here for two years now. Why would anyone be sending me mail here?"

"I don't know," Felix said. "But I'll go get it for you."

Maria was so engrossed in Mama's pie that she almost forgot why Felix had left in the few minutes he was gone. When he came back, he handed her a manila envelope. Her name and this address was written on it in block letters, but the return address seemed to be some kind of law firm. The name looked familiar, but it took her several seconds to place it. When she did, her smile disappeared.

"What's wrong?" Papa asked.

"Nothing," Maria said, trying to put a fake smile on her face. "It's nothing. Nothing to worry about. Just… a letter from someone I didn't expect to ever hear from again. Is there someplace I can go where I can read this in private?"

"You can use our bedroom, if you want," Mama said.

"Thanks." Maria stood up.

"Did you want me to…?" Kevin started to ask.

"Um, yes. Could you? For all I know this might be something you need to see, too."

"Are you sure you're okay?" Ramon asked. "You look like you've seen a ghost."

You're not far off, Maria thought, but she kept up the fake smile and said everything was fine. Kevin followed her down the hall to her parents' bedroom and closed the door behind them. Maria plopped down on her parents' bed, staring at the envelope.

"Okay, tell me what's wrong," Kevin said. "And stop with the 'I'm fine' crap. You know you can't pull that on me."

"Look at the return address," Maria said, handing him the envelope. Kevin looked and shrugged.

"Okay? I'm not sure what the big deal is."

"I wouldn't know either if I hadn't heard Merchant mention it casually in conversation soon after we got back from the islands. That law firm? It's the one that represented Susan Laramie."

"Oh," Kevin said as he sat down next to her. "Are you sure that's something you want to open?"

"Not like I have much of a choice."

"You do, though."

"I'm still not sure if I'm ready to face her. Dead or not."

"How about this? I'll open it and read it for you. Then I'll tell you if it's something I think you should look at. Do you trust me with that?"

Maria smiled. "Of course I do." She handed him the envelope. "Go for it."

Kevin made a big comical flourish of opening up the envelope and pulling out the single sheet of notebook paper that was inside.

Whatever it was, the letter was handwritten in a distinctly girly hand. Kevin held the paper in such a way that she couldn't see it as he read it. For all of three seconds, a smile stayed on his face. Then it abruptly vanished.

"What?" Maria asked. "What is it?"

"Just… just hold on, okay?" He finished reading the letter in silence, his mouth dropping open slightly as he read. When he finally finished, he glanced at her, then went back to read it a second time.

"Kevin?" Maria asked.

"Shit," Kevin said quietly. "Oh, son of a shit-biscuit."

"Kevin, tell me. What is it?"

"Uh, you need to read this yourself."

"You can't just summarize?"

"No. You… you have to read this." He seemed reluctant to hand it over to her, though. Finally, Maria yanked it out of his hands and read the first line for herself.

Hello, Maria. This is Susan Laramie, although you knew me as Diane Mercer. And if you are reading this, then I am dead.

Maria looked up at Kevin. "What the hell?"

"Keep reading."

It took an enormous amount of personal willpower, but she did.

My best guess would be that someone made it look like an accident or a suicide. But I'm telling you straight up that I wouldn't kill myself. At least not before I had spoken to you. I'm writing this letter and giving it to one of my lawyers that I trust with the instruction that it only gets sent if I die.

I had hoped to tell you this in person, because I know you have no reason at all to trust me. I don't blame you. Maybe if we talk in person, you'll see in my eyes that I'm not lying. I hope that's what happens. I hope you never see this.

Please believe me when I tell you this. I want to make things right. I heard about your leg, and I know you probably think it's partly my fault. I think so too. I'm saying this to try to make amends.

Following Dave's death (the man you knew as Murphy), I was too shocked to pay much attention to what was happening other than the giant shark in the water. It wasn't until later, when I was in prison and able to see all the charges against me, that I realized something was wrong. I freely admit that everything I was charged with, I did.

Except one.

Maria lowered the letter. "I don't know if I want to know."

Kevin gently pushed the letter back up. "No, you definitely don't want to know. But you have to." Maria closed her eyes for a few seconds, took some deep breaths, and then kept reading.

The people who convinced us to do this gave us the bomb to put on the Tetsuo Maru. *And that was the only bomb they gave us. But you already know that wasn't the only explosion that day. There was another on the Cameron that took out the engines. But neither me nor Dave did that.*

I hope you understand what I'm saying. There…

Maria stopped reading. She understood exactly what Laramie was saying. But it couldn't be true. The woman had to be lying from beyond the grave.

"Oh God," Maria said quietly. "Kevin, what are we going to do?"

"I don't know."

After a few more seconds, Maria forced herself to read the last two sentences. Then she read it again. And again. And again.

I hope you understand what I'm saying. There was someone else on the Cameron *that day that planted the bomb.*

Someone else on your crew was a traitor.

EPILOGUE

On paper, in as much as the company existed on paper at all, Paperclip Unlimited only had three physical assets: a warehouse in Illinois, a cargo freighter on the Atlantic, and a small two-prop plane that never seemed to be where official paperwork claimed it was. Should anyone ever take enough interest in the company to look for such a paper trail, they might come to the conclusion that Paperclip was a dummy corporation, considering its sole purpose appeared to be that it owned smaller companies, and was in turn owned by a much larger company. It looked to all the world as though it were inconsequential.

This was, of course, by design. The company's two owners, while having a stake in many multi-billion dollar corporations around the world, considered Paperclip Unlimited to be their primary business. It was from there that the two oversaw the rest of their empire. And it was in that single warehouse, looking to the rest of the world as though it were inconsequential and practically abandoned, that they did their primary planning.

"When are we going to put in stairs?" Simon whined as he came down the ladder behind Cindy. Not that Simon and Cindy were their actual names, but Cindy couldn't help but feel like they'd worn these personas long enough that they fit well, like if they were forced to vanish off the radar and live off just one of their identities for the rest of their lives, these were the identities they would choose.

"When you learn to build stairs yourself," Cindy said. That was one part she didn't like about these personas. The bickering. It was so unlike them otherwise, and yet it was seeping into their everyday interactions now even when they were pretending to be other people.

She wasn't kidding about the stairs, though. The room they had entered was below the warehouse, only accessible from a locked hatch behind a dust-covered stack of boxes full of 90's era computer parts. If they wanted a staircase instead of a ladder to get in here, they would need to hire someone from the outside. And then, when those people were finished, Cindy and Simon would have to have them killed. Not that Cindy actually had a problem with a little murder now and then. She just didn't want to expend the effort on something that didn't immediately further their goals. And murder investigations could get so messy. Not everyone's death was as easy to fake as a suicide as Susan Laramie's had been.

"Why do we even need to be here?" Simon asked. "Shouldn't we be out prepping the next part?"

"Think for a minute, Simon," Cindy said. "Think of your beloved theory. If this were fiction, what would we be here for?"

Simon appeared to give this serious thought. "Well, I'm not sure if this were a TV show or book, but if we were in a movie? This would be the short scene after the credits that gives the audience hints of what to expect in upcoming movies."

"Well, there you go then," Cindy said. "I guess that must be why we're here." Simon looked satisfied with this. In truth, Cindy was still far from admitting that they were fictitious, but Simon had been right about their situations enough times that Cindy wouldn't dismiss the possibility out of hand. She tried to ignore any existential dilemma this would cause by telling herself that her brother was simply certifiably insane. And that probably wouldn't be far off from the truth. He was the unpredictable one, after all. She was the calm and cool one, the one who kept their endeavor on track.

While Simon puttered around in various filing cabinets looking at paperwork, Cindy went over to the room's far wall, with its massive corkboard holding a map of the world. Let Simon believe they were here for whatever fictional reason, but Cindy had wanted to come because she felt a base need to update the map. Not that the map mattered anymore this late in the game, but map had been her cornerstone from the moment they had taken up their mission, and it felt wrong to leave it here all alone and uncorrected.

There was a small jar of pins with various colored heads on a table nearby, and Cindy rooted through it until she found a red one. Then she went back to the map and stared at the representation of their handiwork. Years of work, going all the way back to long before the two of them had been born, and it was finally in the end stages.

There were pins sticking in places throughout the entire map, but the vast majority of them were white. Each and every white pin represented some project that fell under Paperclip Unlimited's purview, all of them either stalled out or too far from completion. Almost all of them, with just a few exceptions, were in some body of water. One hundred and thirteen white pins in all. At this late stage, most of them were no longer of any use to Cindy.

In this sea of white, though, three colors stood out. At the moment, there was only a single red pin placed directly over El Bajo Seamount in the Sea of Cortez. A project that was over with and had finished its part to play in things to come.

There were four yellow pins in the map. One had been stuck in Isla Niña in the Galápagos Archipelago. That was the one Cindy needed to update. She removed the yellow pin and replaced it with the red one she had taken from the jar. They'd gotten what they needed from there.

Cindy smiled as she found the three remaining yellow pins, touching each one as though to assure her that those projects were still ready to be tested. One in the Hawaiian Islands, likely the next one that come to public light. One in the Great Lakes. And one on the Great Barrier Reef.

They were all wondrous. They were all special. They were all her babies, just like Teddy Bear and Call It George had been.

Out of the entire map, there was only one pin that was not white, red, or yellow. There was a single green pin in the Atlantic Ocean. This particular map didn't show the ocean topography, but if it had, it would show that the pin was the Mariana Trench, the deepest part of the ocean, a place so far below the surface of the world that no human had ever been able to travel all the way to the bottom.

Cindy caressed the green pin. That was the end, the final part of everything she and her brother had worked toward for their entire lives. As she touched it, Cindy sang softly to herself, allowing a wicked smile to grow on her lips.

"There's a hole, there's a hole, there's a hole in the bottom of the sea."

But unlike the song, the creature in the hole was far, far worse than a frog. And within the coming months, the world would finally see it.

Maria Quintero and Kevin Hoyt will return in
Assassin's Pod

CHECK OUT OTHER GREAT DEEP SEA THRILLERS

SEA RAPTOR
by John J. Rust

From terrorist hunter to monster hunter! Jack Rastun was a decorated U.S. Army Ranger, until an unfortunate incident forced him out of the service. He is soon hired by the Foundation for Undocumented Biological Investigation and given a new mission, to search for cryptids, creatures whose existence has not been proven by mainstream science. Teaming up with the daring and beautiful wildlife photographer Karen Thatcher, they must stop a sea monster's deadly rampage along the Jersey Shore. But that's not the only danger Rastun faces. A group of murderous animal smugglers also want the creature. Rastun must utilize every skill learned from years of fighting, otherwise, his first mission for the FUBI might very well be his last.

OCEAN'S HAMMER
by D.J. Goodman

Something strange is happening in the Sea of Cortez. Whales are beaching for no apparent reason and the local hammerhead shark population, previously believed to be fished to extinction, has suddenly reappeared. Marine biologists Maria Quintero and Kevin Hoyt have come to investigate with a television producer in tow, hoping to get footage that will land them a reality TV show. The plan is to have a stand-off against a notorious illegal shark-fishing captain and then go home.

Things are not going according to plan.

There is something new in the waters of the Sea of Cortez. Something smart. Something huge. Something that has its own plans for Quintero and Hoyt.

CHECK OUT OTHER GREAT DEEP SEA THRILLERS

MEGATOOTH
by Viktor Zarkov

When the death rate of sperm whales rises dramatically, a well-respected environmental activist puts together a ragtag team to hit the high seas to investigate the matter. They suspect that the deaths are due to poachers and they are all driven by a need for justice.

Elsewhere, an experimental government vessel is enhancing deep sea mining equipment. They see one of these dead whales up close and personal...and are fairly certain that it wasn't poachers that killed it.

Both of these teams are about to discover that poachers are the least of their worries. There is something hunting the whales...

Something big
Something prehistoric.
Something terrifying.
MEGATOOTH!

BLOOD CRUISE
by Jake Bible

Ben Clow's plans are set. Drop off kids, pick up girlfriend, head to the marina, and hop on best friend's cruiser for a weekend of fun at sea. But Ben's happy plans are about to be changed by a tentacled horror that lurks beneath the waves.

International crime lords! Deep cover black ops agents! A ravenous, bloodsucking monster! A storm of evil and danger conspire to turn Ben Clow's vacation from a fun ocean getaway into a nightmare of a Blood Cruise!

CHECK OUT OTHER GREAT DEEP SEA THRILLERS

www.ingramcontent.com/pod-product-compliance
Lightning Source LLC
Chambersburg PA
CBHW032145170626
46808CB00006B/2380